I0663777

Planet Evë Series

The Ancient Five

Derek A Morrison

Planet Evë
Series:

The
Anient Five

Tessr
Games

Book Of
Megi

Pillars
Of Light

Clash Of
Spells

Realm Of
Darkness

The Ultimate
Plan

Lance's
War

The Final
Battle

Derek A Morrison was born and raised in Sidney, Nebraska. After graduating high school in May of 2010, he moved to Colorado where he currently resides with his family. Derek has a strong passion for writing and enjoys every moment of it. He also enjoys watching TV shows, being outside, and spending time with his family. "Always believe in yourself and never give up what drives that belief."

~Derek A Morrison

Table of Contents

Prologue:

The End Is Only The Beginning

Gong....gong, the bell rang. Blue skies covered above. The birds were out singing and the flowers were all in bloom. Even the school was teaching lessons outside. The people of Azel were enjoying this beautiful afternoon when everything changed as a loud, *crack,* rang throughout the city, silencing everything in its path.

Crack, came the noise again. The noise seemingly to have come from the center of Azel; from King Evergreen's castle. *Crack, crack*, continued to echo down from within the castle walls.

While the citizens of Azel were outside listening to the cracking, the monks of Azel were being murdered in the Chamber of Light.

"Please have mercy! You don't know what you're doing," cried Father Izea, lying on the floor backed up against a wall. Father Izea was one of the most honorable and noble monks, devoting his entire life to the Light.

"Oh, but I do," said a man with a soul dark as night as one of his followers kills the last remaining monk, besides Father Izea. "Now, where are the orbs?" the man asked.

"What orbs?" Father Izea asked with confusion.

"What orbs? Try THE ELEMENTAL ORBS!" the man screamed at Father Izea as he crouched down next to him, grasping a bloody knife in his left hand, and a secret map of King Evergreen's castle in his right.

"I.... I don't know what you're talking about," Father Izea whimpered in fear.

"No, that is not the right answer Father," the man said as he lifted the knife. Just as the man was about to kill Father Izea, a red stone went rolling out of the Father's pocket. The man quickly grabbed the stone, then the bag from which it came from. Inside were other kinds of stones; in quantities. "It's.... it's....," the man started to say.

"It's the Elemental Orbs, Mr. Anders. Take a good look at them, because it will be your last," sounded a deep yet powerful voice from the doorway. It was King Evergreen, armed for battle. He took only a few steps into the chamber to allow his guards entrance to the room, as well as to hopefully strike fear into Mr. Anders.

Mr. Anders started chuckling, "You really think you can stop me?" He quickly pulled himself and Father Izea up, holding the knife back up against Father Izea's neck.

"'The Chosen One will'," one of the guards said, trying not to show fear.

"'The Chosen One'?" Mr. Anders asked. "Ha! I'm taking care of that as we speak." Silence filled the room.

"You're a monster," King Evergreen said, preparing to fight.

"Now now your highness," Mr. Anders started out. "We wouldn't want anything bad to happen to you, now would we?"

"Let go of the orbs, Christopher!" King Evergreen demanded.

"Try me," Mr. Anders snarled as he pushed Father Izea into King Evergreen and pulled out a yellow stone. Instantly, he threw it on the floor and stepped on it. A very small cloud of dark, cosmic energy appeared. All of a sudden, a large cracking noise came from below, moving the ground under everyone enough to make them stumble a bit. The cloud suddenly disappeared, leaving nothing but silence. Pure silence.

"Wha....wha....what was that cracking?" asked one of the guards with a bit of concern in his voice.

"What was that cloud?" asked another. Just as the guard stopped asking his question, the ground started shaking so bad that the Chamber of Light started falling apart. Mr. Anders grabbed Father Izea again and started towards the doorway slowly.

"If anyone tries to stop me, I'll kill him on the spot," he threatened.

"Stand down!" shouted the King. Mr. Anders quickly led Father Izea and himself to the exit. While doing so, the King and his guards quickly moved out of Mr. Ander's way. With the ground shaking more and more violently, the King began to show fear and concern for his great city. When the two got to the exit, he threw Father Izea onto the floor and just like that, Mr. Anders was gone.

"Quick, after him!" shouted King Evergreen's head guard. All of the guards stumbled out of the room, trying not to fall in their pursuit of Mr. Anders.

"Father, what's going on?" King Evergreen asked as he quickly hurried over to Father Izea, trying not to trip over the dead monks.

"The worst thing imaginable," he started to say as the king helped him up, "the entire city is about to fall completely out of the sky."

Meanwhile, things outside weren't looking too good either. A large explosion came from the Northwest side of the castle; the king's chambers. As all of the guards went rushing inside, Mr. Anders snuck out of the castle and headed towards the communication tower, located in sector B-3. Outside the castle, the ground seemed to have stopped shaking. The rest of the city slowly became silent. Some buildings were partially destroyed and a few were on fire.

Just as Mr. Anders got to the communication tower, the ground started shaking again, but this time much worse. Large cracking noises could be heard across the city, all coming from sector D in the Southwest. After a short time of cracking noises, sectors D-2 and D-3 started to break off and fall towards the surface. Pure chaos seemed to flood the entire city.

Mere seconds after D-2, and D-3 had fallen, the rest of sector D (which included sectors D-1, D-4, and D-5) joined in the plummet to the ground. By time the entire D sector started to fall, Mr. Anders had barely arrived at the top of the communication tower. Soon after, sector B-3 started to fall as well. Mr. Anders then pulled out a large sphere from inside his coat.

"Moonshiar," he said. Instantly, it started glowing red. He threw it on the ground below him. When it broke open, red smoke appeared and surrounded him.

"Three down, two to go," Mr. Anders chuckled as the smoke reached his face. The smoke quickly lifted and Mr. Anders was gone. As the once floating city fell to its doom, it disappeared into a dark storm that was quickly heading towards the falling city.

Chapter One:

Lost In The Woods

"We are so going to get caught," Kim said.

"No we won't. I found the perfect way in and out," replied Drake as they hid in the shadows, waiting. As soon as the coast was clear, Drake darted for the other side of the street.

"Drake..." Kim quietly said to herself as Drake disappeared into the shadows. Kim had always admired Drake; the way he never changed his semi short brown hair, or how his bright blue eyes shined in the sun. He was about 5'6", just a little bit taller than her, which she adored. Kim herself had long burgundy red hair that fell about half way down her back. Her hazel eyes changed colors with her mood, which was definitely a unique feature about her.

After heaving a big sigh, she soon joined Drake. The two lurked in the shadows all the way to the border of the city. Walking along the outer wall, a small opening appeared. It looked like someone had blown into the city but there was no rubble.

"You sure you know what you're doing?"

"Of course," Drake said with delight in his voice as he walked through the hole onto the green grass ahead. "What's the worst thing that could happen?" he asked as Kim joined him. The greenest grass seemed to grow all around the wall, with the forest only one-fourth of a clik away. "Come on!" Drake shouted, as he took off running through the field towards the forest.

"Drake, wait up!" Kim shouted as she tried to keep up. Just as she got to the forest line, she stopped and looked back. Taking in the gorgeous view only for a moment, Kim took a deep breath and headed into the forest. As she slowly walked further and further, the trance of the forest took hold of her. Mesmerized by the scenery around her, Kim didn't realize that Drake was sneaking up on her.

"Boo," he said, from right behind her.

"Aaaa!" Kim screamed. "What the heck Drake?"

Drake, with a smug smile on his face started laughing. The laughter became contagious as Kim started to laugh too. As the two best friends stood there laughing, something was creeping up on them and fast. There was a small noise, almost like twigs breaking that startled the two teens.

"What was that?" Kim asked, slightly concerned.

"I don't know," Drake said as he continued laughing.

"I'm serious Drake!" said Kim as she punched Drake in the left arm.

"I didn't hear anyth…" Drake started to speak until he was interrupted with a rustling noise in the trees in front of him.

"I don't like it here Drake. Let's go back!" Kim demanded, trying to act brave yet trying to cuddle under Drake's arms at the same time.

"It….iiiit….it was probably just the wind," Drake said half nervous. A pair of bright violet eyes suddenly appeared in front of Drake and Kim.

"Run!" they both screamed at each other. They turned around and booked it, not knowing that that would just make things even worse. Drake and Kim thought they were heading back towards safety when they were actually running parallel with the field and heading towards a stream. When they arrived at the stream, they stopped to catch their breath. Drake quickly looked around to see if the eyes were still in sight. Kim looked too. They saw nothing. No eyes, no noise, no nothing. All they could hear was their own shortness of breath and the stream below.

"Let's get out of here," Drake said.

"I agree!" Kim replied without hesitation. After waiting a moment to catch their breath, they were both about ready to leave when a rare silver wolf jumped in front of them from out of nowhere. "Aaaaaaaa!" Kim screamed loudly.

"I'll protect you!" Drake said with confidence, holding Kim behind him.

"It has been ages since I've seen someone like you way out here," came a strange voice inside Drake's head.

"What?" Drake thought to himself.

"Just stand still so I can devour you easily," the strange voice said. Drake was looking right at the wolf when he realized that it was the wolf's voice he could hear inside his head. The wolf was about to attack when another silver wolf jumped in front of Drake and Kim, but this one seemed to be there to protect them. The wolf turned its head towards Drake and Kim and instantly, he noticed the same bright violet eyes as before.

"Run!" said a teenage voice inside Drake's head.

Drake grabbed Kim and started running away from the two wolves, wondering why he was hearing voices other than his own. Had he gone mad? Did he catch a disease or something out in the forest? Whatever was going on, things were about to get even stranger. Drake looked back to see what was happening and before his very own eyes, the violet eyed wolf transformed into a great long-horn deer. Baffled by this sight, Drake quickly turned around and continued running.

Not knowing that Drake had stopped to see what was happening, Kim soon found herself in the field and found the opening they came in through.

"Never again Drake," she finally said after she caught her breath. There was no response. "Drake?" she asked as she turned around. No one was behind her. Drake was now officially alone in the forest.

As Kim sprinted back to the city to get help to find Drake, Drake was still looking for Kim.

"Kim!" Drake shouted, "Kim? I get it! You want to scare me because I scared you! I get it." Drake stood against a big, tall tree listening to the silence that seemed to have fallen across the forest. Drake's heart dropped as he began to realize he was all alone; lost in a place where he had no clue which way was which. Wandering and trying to find his home, darkness was coming quickly. Little did Drake know he was getting further and further from home.

Drake was always an adventurous young boy. He spent most of his days getting into trouble and his nights reading all the books in the Library Hall. He thought for a moment and remembered reading about how to build a fire and quickly did.

After gathering sticks for the fire and berries for food, it was time to eat and rest. Drake, almost curling up with the fire, stared up at the stars above. He had so many questions. Was Kim safe? Did she make it back to the city? Was his dad looking for him? Was his mother worried sick? Then he started wondering about other questions. What was that thing that had helped him? Was he really hearing other voices inside his head? Did he catch something? Was he going insane? A ruffling noise slowly caught Drake's attention. He quickly shot up. In the distance, the ruffling noise got louder and was coming right at him.

"Kim?" he stuttered as he rose to his feet and grabbed a stick from the fire. He pointed the flames towards the noise to see what was making it. The noise ceased and the bright violet eyes appeared. Drake took a step back.

"Wait," said a teenage voice in Drake's head. "I'm not going to hurt you."

"You....you're not?" Drake said nervously. The eyes slowly pulled forward revealing a brown horse in the light.

"Nope," the teenage voice paused. "You must be 'The Chosen One'," exclaimed the voice, causing Drake to cover his ears, accidently dropping the lit stick. He looked at the horse; now jumping and kicking as though it was excited. In a matter of seconds, the "excited" horse transformed from a horse to a silver wolf. Drake almost exploded with fear.

"WHAT ARE YOU!?" Drake screamed so loud that the dead could have heard him. The now "excited" wolf immediately stopped, staring at Drake.

"Why, I'm a Seî," the teenage voice said proudly.

"A what?" Drake asked.

"A Seî, silly."

"This voice I hear, is it your voice?" Drake asked with a little bit of confidence in his voice.

"Yes, they're my thoughts. Try thinking your next question instead of speaking it. It's a lot of fun!"

"Why can I hear your thoughts?" Drake thought.

"It's called telepathy."

"Te-what?" Drake asked in thought.

"Telepathy." the teenage voice said. "It's the power to communicate through thoughts."

"Why can I hear your thoughts?"

"I...I...I Don't know," the teenage voice said a bit shocked. "No one has ever been able to hear my thoughts before. It's always been the creature's thought I could hear." There was a brief pause as Drake thought to himself for a moment.

"Do you have a name?" Drake finally asked after taking a moment to think.

"No," the teenage voice thought sadly.

"How about I call you Zack?"

"I LOVE IT!!"

"Well I need to get some rest. It's late and I have to be up early."

"Can I stay with you for tonight? It's kinda lonely out here sometimes." Zack asked.

"You're seriously not going to hurt me, are you?"

"No, I'm not," the teenage voice thought in a serious tone. Drake thought to himself that he must be telling the truth or he would have attacked already.

"I can," Zack started to say but was interrupted by a yawn, "I can help you find your way home." He stated as he walked over to Drake. The warm fur of Zack's coat started to make Drake feel nice and warm.

"Alright. Now, it's bedtime." Drake put out the fire and lay down against a big tree. Zack walked over to where Drake was laying.

"Goodnight Zack," Drake said as he closed his eyes.

"Goodnight….friend," Zack said as he laid his head down and closed his eyes.

Drake's eyes shot open. The sky was a light pink as the sun rose. Zack was still fast asleep. Drake couldn't fall back to sleep so he watched as the stars faded away and blue covered the sky above. Zack soon let out a large yawn, opened his eyes, and stretched as he got up.

"Ready?" he thought eagerly.

"You just got up and you're ready to go already?" Drake responded.

"Well yeah. Aren't you?"

Drake stood up, took a big yawn, and said, "Yeah, I guess." As the sun slowly rose, Drake's feelings toward Zack slowly grew from a little bit nervous to totally trustworthy. After hours of walking around, trying to escape the forest, Drake and Zack decided to take a short rest. "What's that?" Drake asked as he pointed to two leaning trees that looked like they shaped a doorway in the distance.

"I don't know," thought Zack. The two got up and walked over to the leaning trees doorway. They walked around and through it. Nothing weird or out of the ordinary happened. It was just two trees that formed the doorway. Drake looked harder and noticed something else. Off in the distance, hidden behind the shadows of the trees ahead was an old stone doorway a few inches taller and a few inches wider than Drake.

The two walked up to the doorway. While examining the doorway, Drake noticed a weird symbol carefully carved into a stone at the top of the doorway. The symbol consisted of three circles and two lines. Drake looked at the symbol for a moment. He swore to himself that he had read somewhere that the symbol he was looking at was the ancient Tërcerlin symbol. Drake slowly ran his fingers across the symbol. Just then, the symbol started to glow a deep red color. At the same time, searing pain shot through his left hand. Drake screamed in pain as he held the top of his hand, trying to reduce the pain.

"What's wrong?" Zack thought.

"My hand," he started to say but was interrupted by another shot of pain. Shortly, the pain reduced and Drake was able to finish, "My hand feels like it is on fire!"

"Let me see," Zack offered to help. Just as Drake was about to show Zack his hand, a third shot of pain raced through this hand. This time, it hurt so bad that Drake let out a cry of pure agony that shattered the silence around them. Drake fell to his knees. Drake had never felt a pain like this before. It was almost like the sun itself was burning into his skin. As the pain went away, Drake finally caught his breath. As soon as the pain was completely gone, the symbol stopped glowing. Drake slowly got up and looked at his hand, revealing the same symbol as on the doorway, burned into the top of his left hand.

"What the?" Drake said as he looked closer at it. "Ouch!" he yelped as he touched it. The skin was still tender from whatever just happened. Drake looked at the stone doorway and noticed it became an actual doorway with a door inside.

"Let's get out of here!" Zack thought, starting to worry. Drake was just about to agree when some kind of force told Drake to open the door, and he did. It was a long dark hallway. Drake started to enter the hallway as Zack transformed into a phoenix, (only located in the Eastern Mountains) and followed right behind Drake. When it got almost too dark to see, Zack turned up the light by setting himself on fire.

"Doesn't that hurt?" Drake asked.

"No, not really," replied Zack. As the two got deeper into the hallway, a faint light appeared and started to get closer. Before they knew it, they were standing in the doorway to a room. There were books and scrolls all along the walls, a table with chairs in the middle of the room, and a giant mirror on the opposite side of the room. Candles of all shapes, sizes, and color were lit and scattered across the room.

"What is this place?" Drake thought to himself as he started to look around. He had never seen a place like this before.

"Who goes there?" a voice asked from somewhere inside the room.

"My name is Drake and this is my friend Zack. I'm sorry to have bothered you. We are lost and looking for directions. Is there any way you could help us?"

"Sure," the voice said, "one moment." Then silence. Moments past and no one made a sound. "Orlo casee a," the voice finally said and a man in a monk looking robe appeared in front of the mirror. "Why hello, and welcome to the Lost Library."

"I've read about this place before, but I would have never imagined it would be real," Drake said in ah.

"Oh no, this place is very real," the man replied, "well Drake and Zack, it's a pleasure to meet you both. My name is Father John and I am the protector of the Lost Library."

"Pleasure to meet you too Father John," Drake said as he stuck his hand out. As Father John grabbed Drake's hand, he noticed the Tërcerlin symbol burned into his skin.

"You're....you're....you're 'The Chosen One'!" Father John said with pure shock and delight.

"Wait!" Drake said. "Wait, wait, wait, you're telling me that I'm 'THE Chosen One'? As in the one who is supposed to save the universe from Darkness?"

"Yes," Father John answered. Drake started laughing. Father John looked confused.

"I must be dreaming," Drake finally said as he finished laughing.

"Look at this mirror and tell me that you're dreaming," Father John said as he walked to the mirror. Drake slowly walked to the mirror as well. He gazed upon it for a moment.

"All I see is myself," Drake said, trying to sound dumb.

"Look again," Father John said determinedly. Drake looked at the mirror again, but this time closer and harder. Images appeared of chaos. Pain, blood, and death seemed to scatter across Evë.

"No, this…. this can't be!" Drake said as he took a few steps back. Images of buildings on fire and people dying started to make Drake cry. All of a sudden, Jewel City, his home appeared blazing in flames and death scattering across its streets. "No, this is all just a dream!" Drake screamed as he took off, running out of the room, through the hallway, and back into the forest.

"Danger lies ahead of him. Quickly go! Help him as much as you can," Father John told Zack.

"I will!" Zack thought as he hurried over to the entrance. Father John began to smile. Zack quickly transformed into a silver wolf and hurried out of the room. Father John's smile grew because he knew 'The Chosen One' had finally been found.

Chapter Two:

Only A Dream

Drake was freaking out like never before as he darted through the forest, alone. Before he knew it, he was standing in the grassy field. After stopping to catch his breath, Drake smelled something odd. It almost had a burning smell to it, like something was on fire. He looked around and noticed pitch black smoke coming from the northwest part of the city. Drake dashed towards the city's wall. As he made his way through the city towards his home, the smell of burning became stronger. He was about six blocks from his home when he realized something was wrong. Where was everyone? From the moment Drake walked into the city he realized there wasn't a single person in sight. He slowly walked on. 'What's going on?" was the only thing racing through Drake's mind.

He suddenly took off running only to come to a complete stop two blocks later. His entire apartment building was on fire. He looked around for his parents, neighbors, friends, anyone but there was again no one in sight. It seemed like the entire city was evacuated or something. Drake took a deep breath and ran into the burning building.

Hurrying and trying to avoid the fire, Drake finally reached the stairs. After getting to the second floor, he had to crouch low to find his apartment due to the amount of smoke in the air. Shortly afterwards, he found his apartment, 217. Without checking the door, Drake kicked the door in, revealing most of his home in flames.

"Mom? Dad?" Drake screamed as he ran through the apartment looking for them. No one seemed to be home, which made him relax a little.

Drake looked in every room for his parents just in case. The last room he checked was his own. Drake kicked the door in as hard as he could. Due to the pressure and lack of oxygen building up inside the room, a fireball immediately formed and shot itself right at Drake.

Drake shot up from his bed. He quickly looked around to find his room perfectly fine and his mother right next to him.

"There, there honey, you're alright," she said softly. Drake was panting and sweating like a river.

"But you," Drake paused, "and the house." He paused again. He pulled his hands out from under the covers, nothing.

"That must have been one bad nightmare you were having."

"Nightmare?" He asked.

"Well yeah, you were talking in your sleep and thrashing about like you were running from something. I tried to wake you up but no matter how hard I tried, you just wouldn't wake up." She paused for a moment to catch her breath. "What was your nightmare about?"

"Our entire apartment was on fire," was all Drake could say.

"Well the sun isn't up yet so go back to sleep."

"Alright. Night mom."

"Night Drake," she said as she got up, kissed Drake's forehead, and left the room, shutting off the light and closing the door behind her. Drake was lost and confused but finally accepted the simple fact that all of the craziness was really a dream or nightmare. He laid back down, turned over, and went back to sleep, not truly realizing what was about to happen. Or that Father John was standing in the shadows, smiling.

Drake's eyes popped open. Light was shining into his room from outside. It was definitely day-time now. Drake got up and smelled something odd, almost like sweat. He smelt himself and boy, did he smell bad. Usually Drake would take cold showers but this time, he decided to take a shower so hot that there was a blanket of steam covering the ceiling of the bathroom. Something felt wrong to Drake. His "nightmare" replayed over and over again. A searing pain suddenly raced through his left hand, forcing him to let out a terrible scream, so loud that his mother came rushing to the door.

"Drake? You okay? What's going on in there?" she asked as she tried to open the door only to find it was locked. Drake fell to his knees, holding his left hand. As he fell he accidently turned the cold water all the way up, hitting the knob with his hip. Steam rolled off Drake's hand as he placed it under the water, hoping it would cool off his hand. In matter of seconds, the pain stopped. Drake, still holding his hand, slowly rose.

"Yeah, I'm fine," he said as he shut off the water.

"What happened?" his mother asked.

"Oh, the water just got extremely hot all of a sudden," he lied. He looked closely at his hand but there was nothing there.

"Oh okay," his mother said through the door. "Well, breakfast is almost ready."

"Okay mom," Drake told her as he started drying off and getting dressed. The tall yet skinny woman sat across from Drake, watching him eat. Her long, snow white hair was pulled up into a bow (the way she looked every morning), and her deep blue eyes glimmered in the light. She had a bit of concern on her face as she watched her son eating his French toast, eggs, and bacon for breakfast. Drake, noticing the hint of concern on his mother's face, started to wonder about himself as well. He'd suddenly realized he had just started on his third helpings of all three breakfast items. The last time Drake even had second helpings was when he was seven years old, just before Drake had to have braces.

"Thanks for breakfast mom," he told her as he placed his dishes in the sink.

"You're welcome," she replied, still concerned for her child. After breakfast, Drake spent the rest of the day inside his room, sleeping. Little did Drake know, things were about to get even worse.

While asleep, Drake's "nightmare" continued. It started off with Drake running out of his burning home.

"Mom? Dad? Where are you?" Drake screamed, hoping for some kind of response. The only sound he heard was the fire roaring behind him. Drake started to freak out. Fire could be seen all over the city and buildings were beginning to collapse. In the distance he saw a girl, around his age, covered in blood, bruises, and torn clothes standing in front of a flaming building. "Hello?" Drake shouted at her. "Hey, can you hear me?" She just stood there. He started walking towards her and when he was about three-fourths of the way there, the girl turned, looked at him, and took off running. "Wait!" Drake shouted as he took off after the girl. She ran to the end of the street and turned. Drake ran as fast as he could, and when he got to the end of the street, he couldn't find her.

Suddenly, he spotted the same girl, standing in front of a collapsed apartment building, staring at him. He took off running towards her again and like last time, when he got close, the girl took off running again.

This routine continued for several blocks, and soon Drake was catching his breath in front of the library. Drake looked around and saw the girl at the top of the stairs, in front of the entrance to the library. As soon as he spotted her, she went running inside. After catching his breath, he entered the library with caution. While inside, everything seemed normal, except for the fact that no one was around and partially destroyed. As Drake walked through the library, he noticed the Tërcerlin symbol scattered throughout the library. While completely confused, a Tërcerlin symbol started glowing on a spine of an old book as Drake walked past it. He stopped and pulled the book from the shelf, walked to the closest table and sat down. He took a deep breath and opened the book. Nothing. He went through page after page of blank pages until he stopped on the only one with anything on it; a Tёrcerlin symbol right in the center. It started glowing like the spine did only this one grew brighter and brighter, blinding him. Drake couldn't see anything and suddenly he was sucked into the light.

Drake slowly opened his eyes to find himself lying on a lush green hill. He slowly got up and looked around seeing only rolling hills upon hills stretching on for miles in all directions. Things were starting to get really weird, and in the faint distance Drake heard a small noise. It sounded like someone screaming from above him. The sound became louder, as if someone was falling. In a very short time, the one person became several people screaming. A small shape started to appear through the clouds ahead. The figure grew bigger and Drake slowly realized that it was a piece of rock; a very large piece of rock. As the rock kept falling, Drake noticed buildings and people on the very top of the rock. He stood there helpless, watching these people fall to their deaths. When the rock hit the ground, another shape appeared and Drake started to cry as the city of Azel fell around him.

Drake was standing there, frozen with fear, tears streaming down his face. He had absolutely no idea where he was or what was really going on, but he was forced to watch those innocent people die. Not paying attention to the sky above, Drake didn't notice one of the rocks was about to fall right on top of him. He caught a glimpse of the falling rock too late and didn't have time to move let alone run. Drake closed his eyes and covered his head with his arms moments before the rock struck.

Drake sprung into a sitting position, eyes wide open, quickly looking around and realizing he was only having another nightmare.

Later that evening, Drake went for a walk to clear his head. As he walked through the city, he noticed people everywhere. Everyone he knew waved at him or said hello, which put him in a good mood and his mind became completely clear of the nightmares he had. He didn't even realized he arrived at the city wall, and that no one was around. With a clear head, Drake didn't mind being alone. He made his way up into an abandoned building to watch the sun slowly set on the horizon. After the sun finally set, Drake started his walk toward home. But on his way, he found something so interesting that he ran to his best friend's house

as fast as he could instead.

Chapter Three:

Dreams Become Reality

"Hey Kim!" he shouted as he approached her house and noticed her outside.

"Hey, what's up?" she replied.

"Are you doing anything tomorrow?"

"Not that I know of. Why? What's up?"

"I found something huge and I want you to check it out with me."

"No thanks."

"Oh come on." There was a brief pause. "Please?" Kim had kind of liked Drake for years and hearing him say please gave her the idea of finding out if Drake liked her the way she liked him.

"Okay," she finally said. Drake was too excited to contemplate what may be in store for him and Kim, or what was about to happen.

The next morning, Drake and Kim hurried through the city. Kim started to freak out.

"What are we doing?" she asked.

"It's not what are we doing, it's where are we going," Drake responded.

"Okay mister smartass." Drake started to laugh. "Where are we going?"

"We are going outside the city walls," he said slowly.

"NO WAY!" Kim shouted as she stopped dead in her tracks.

"Kim please," Drake said.

"It's completely forbidden for us to leave the city."

"But you told me you wanted an adventure." During Kim's last birthday, the only thing she wanted from Drake was an adventure. Kim was always a bright student; always getting A's and constantly studying. Her parents set such high expectations for her and all she did was meet those expectations but, deep inside, she longed for an adventure.

"We are so going to get caught," Kim finally said.

"No we won't. I found the perfect way in and out," replied Drake as they sat in the shadows, waiting. As soon as the coast is clear, Drake darted for the outer side of the street.

"Drake…." Kim quietly said to herself as Drake disappeared into the shadows. After heaving a big sigh, she soon joined Drake. The two lurked in the shadows all the way to the border of the city. Walking along the outer wall, a small opening appeared. It looked like someone had blown into the city but there was no rubble.

"You sure you know what you're doing?"

"Of course," Drake said with delight in his voice as he walked through the hole onto the green grass ahead. "What's the worst that could happen?" he asked as Kim joined him. The greenest grass seemed to grow all around the outer wall with a forest only one-fourth of a click away. "Come on!" Drake shouted as he took off through the field of grass towards the forest.

"What's wrong?" Kim asked as she caught up with him. "I don't know," he started to tell her. "Something seems….off."

"Off?"

"Yeah. It's really hard to explain," he paused for a moment. "Come on," he said as he continued walking towards the forest. As the two walked into the forest, the trance of the forest took a hold of them.

As the two best friends stood there mesmerized, something was creeping up on them and fast. There was a small noise, almost like twigs breaking that startled the two teens.

"What was that?" Kim asked, slightly concerned.

"I don't know," Drake said sarcastically.

"I'm serious Drake!" said Kim as she punched Drake in the left arm.

"I didn't hear anyth…" Drake started to speak until he was interrupted with a moving noise in the trees in front of him.

"I don't like it here Drake. Let's go back!" demanded Kim, trying to act brave yet trying to cuddle under Drake's arms.

"It…iiiit…it was probably just the wind," Drake said half nervous. A pair of bright violet eyes suddenly appeared in front of Drake and Kim.

"Run!" they both screamed at each other. They turned around and booked it, not knowing that what they just did made things even worse. Drake and Kim thought they were heading back towards safety when they were actually running parallel with the field and heading towards a stream. When they arrived at the stream, they stopped to catch their breath. Drake quickly looked around to see if the eyes were still around. Kim looked too. Nothing. No eyes, no noise, no nothing. All they could hear was the shortness of breath and the stream below.

"Let's get out of here," Drake said.

"I agree!" Kim replied without any hesitation. After waiting a moment to catch their breath, they were both about ready to leave when a rare silver wolf jumped in front of them from out of nowhere. "Aaaaaaaa!" Kim screamed.

"I'll protect you!" Drake said with confidence, holding Kim behind him.

"It has been ages since I've seen someone like you way out here," came a strange voice inside Drake's head.

"What?" Drake thought to himself.

"Just stand still so I can devour you easily," the strange voice said. Drake was looking right at the wolf when he realized that it was the wolf's voice he could hear inside his head. The wolf was about to attack when another silver wolf jumped in front of Drake and Kim but this one seemed to be protecting them. The wolf turned its head towards Drake and Kim and instantly, he noticed the same bright violet eyes as before.

"Run!" came a teenage voice inside Drake's head. Drake grabbed Kim and started running away from the two wolves, wondering why he was hearing voices other than his own. Had he gone mad? Did he catch a disease or something out in the forest? Whatever was going on, things were about to get even stranger. Drake looked back to see what was happening and before his very own eyes, the violet eyed wolf transformed into a great long-horned deer. Baffled by this sight, Drake quickly turned and continued running. While running, Drake started to feel that strange feeling again, the same feeling from the field. Confused about this feeling, Drake soon noticed he had stopped running and Kim was nowhere to be seen.

✧ ✧ ✧ ✧ ✧ ✧ ✧ ✧ ✧ ✧ ✧ ✧

Meanwhile, not knowing that Drake wasn't with her, Kim soon found herself in the field and found the opening they came through.

"Never again Drake," she finally said after she caught her breath. There was no response. "Drake?" she asked as she turned around. No one was behind her. Drake was now officially alone in the forest. As Kim sprinted back to the city to get help to find Drake, Drake was still looking for Kim.

✧ ✧ ✧ ✧ ✧ ✧ ✧ ✧ ✧ ✧ ✧ ✧

"Kim?" Drake shouted. "Kim? Where are you?" Drake stood against a big, tall tree listening to the silence that seemed to have fallen across the forest. Drake's heart dropped. He realized he was all alone; lost in a place where he had no clue which way was which. Wandering and trying to find his home, darkness was coming quick and little did Drake know, he was getting further and further away from home. Drake was always an adventurous young boy. He spent most of his days getting into trouble and his nights reading all the books in the library hall. Because he read so many books Drake knew how to start a fire. After gathering sticks for a fire and berries for food, it was time to rest. Drake, almost curling up with the fire, starred up at the stars above wondering so many questions. Was Kim safe? Did she make it back to the city? Was his dad looking for him? Was his mother worried sick? Then he started wondering about other questions. What was that thing that helped him? Was he really hearing other voice? Did he catch something? Was he going insane? A ruffling noise slowly caught Drake's attention. He quickly shot up and in the distance the ruffling noise got louder and was coming right at him. "Kim?" he stuttered as he rose to his feet grabbing a stick that was half on fire. He pointed the flame towards the noise to see what was making it. The noises seceded and bright violet eyes appeared. Drake took a step back. "Wait," said a teenage voice in Drakes head. "I'm not trying to hurt you."

"You…you're not?" Drake nervously said. The eyes slowly pulled forward, revealing a brown horse in the light.

"No I'm not…Wait!" came the teenage voice again, "You can hear me?" the voice seemed happy.

"Ye…yes?" Drake answered, still very nervous.

"You must be 'The Chosen One'!" screamed the voice inside Drakes head, causing him to cover his ears and accidentally dropping the lit stick, he looked at the horse, now jumping and kicking as though it was excited. In a matter of seconds, this "excited" horse transformed from a horse to a silver wolf, Drake almost exploded with fear.

"What are you!" Drake screamed so loud that the dead could have heard him. The now jumping wolf immediately stopped, staring at Drake.

"Why, I'm a Seî," the teenage voice said proudly.

"A what?" Drake said.

"A Seî, silly," the teenage voice spoke again.

"This voice I hear, is it your voice?" Drake said with a little bit of confidence in his voice.

"Yes, they're my thoughts. Try thinking your next question instead of speaking it."

"Why can I hear your thoughts?" Drake thought.

"It's called telepathy."

"Te-what?" Drake asked.

"Telepathy." the teenage voice said. "It's the power to communicate through thought."

"Why can I hear your thoughts?"

"I...I...I Don't know," the teenage voice said a bit shocked. "No one has ever been able to hear my thoughts before. It's always been the creature's thought I could hear." There was a brief pause as Drake thought to himself for a moment.

"Do you have a name?" Drake finally asked.

"No" the teenage voice thought sadly. "But can I stay with you for tonight? It's kind of lonely out here."

"You're seriously not going to hurt me, are you?"

"No I'm not," the teenage voice said in a serious tone. Drake thought to himself that he must be telling the truth or he would have attacked already.

"I'll call you Zack," Drake said as he picked up the lit stick and placed it back in the fire.

"Zack?" the teenage voice paused for a moment, "I like it!"

"Good but I need some sleep now so I can find my way home tomorrow." Drake put out the fire and laid against a big tree. Zack walked over to where Drake was laying.

"I can," Zack started to say but was interrupted by a yawn. "I can help you find your way home." He walked over next to Drake. The warm fur from Zack's coat started to make Drake feel nice and warm.

"Good night Zack," Drake said as he closed his eyes.

"Good night… Friend," Zack said as he laid his head down and closed his eyes. Just like that, Zack was fast asleep. Drake opened his eyes and starred at the stars above. It was now official. Something definitely seemed off to Drake, almost like he had been in a familiar situation or something. Drake's eyes grew heavy. He must have been really tired. He took a deep sigh, closed his eyes, and off to sleep he went.

Drake's eyes shot open. There was a very light pink color in the sky. Zack was still asleep. Drake couldn't fall back to sleep so he watched as the stars faded away and blue covered above. Zack soon let out a large yawn, opened his eyes, and stretched as he got up.

"Ready?" he thought eagerly.

"You just got up and you're ready to go already?" Drake responded.

"Well yeah. Aren't you?"

Drake stood up, let out a big yawn, and said "Yeah, I guess." As the sun slowly rose, Drake's feeling towards Zack slowly grew from a little bit nervous to totally trustworthy. After hours of walking around, trying to escape the forest, Drake and Zack decided to take a short rest. "What's that?" Drake asked as he pointed to two trees that looked like a doorway in the distance. Drake looked harder and noticed something else. Off in the distance, hidden behind the shadows of the trees ahead was an old stone doorway.

The two walked up to the doorway. It was only a few inches taller and a few inches wider than Drake. While examining the doorway, Drake noticed a weird symbol carefully carved into a stone at the top of the doorway. The symbol consisted of three circles and tow lines. Drake looked at the symbol for a moment. He swore to himself that he had read somewhere that the symbol he was looking at was the ancient Tërcerlin symbol. Drake started to slowly run his fingers across the symbol when the strange feeling appeared again but this time, he knew what was going on and what was about to happen. Drake quickly pulled his had away but he was too late.

The symbol started to glow a deep red color. At the same time, searing pain shot through his left hand. Drake screamed in pain as he covered his left hand, trying to reduce the pain.

"What's wrong!" Zack thought to Drake as he hurried over to him.

"My hand," he started to say but was interrupted by another shot of pain. Shortly, the pain reduced and Drake was able to finish, "My hand feels like it's on fire."

"Let me see," Zack offered to help. Just as Drake was about to show Zack his hand, a third shot of pain raced through his hand. This time, it hurt so bad that Drake let out a cry of pure agony that shattered the silence around them. Drake fell to his knees in pain. As the pain went away, Drake finally caught his breath. As soon as the ache was completely gone, the symbol stopped glowing. Drake slowly got up and pulled back his right hand, revealing the same symbol as the doorway, burned into his skin. Drake looked up at the stone doorway and noticed it became an actual doorway with a door inside.

"Let's get out of here!" Zack thought, starting to worry.

"Not just yet," Drake said. He grabbed the doorknob and opened the door.

It was a long dark hallway. "Can you turn into a phoenix?" Drake asked.

"Sure," responded Zack. He turned into a phoenix and the two entered the hallway. Once it got almost too dark to see, Zack turned up the heat and light by setting himself on fire.

"Doesn't that hurt?" Drake thought.

"No not really," replied Zack. As the two went deeper into the hallway, a faint light appeared and started to get closer. Before they knew it, they were standing in the doorway to a room. There were books and scrolls along the walls, a table with chairs in the middle of the room, and a giant mirror on the opposite end of the room. White candles of all sizes were lit and scattered across the room. Drake started to walk around the room. A strange noise startled Drake and Zack.

"Who's there?" Drake asked.

"Orlo casee a," came a voice from inside the room and a man in a monk looking robe appeared sitting in a chair. The man got up and turned around, facing Drake. "Hello and welcome to the Lost Library."

"THE Lost Library?"

"Yes, and I'm the protector of the Lost Library."

"I'm Drake Shaw," Drake said.

"It's a pleasure to meet you Mr. Drake Shaw. I'm father," the man started to say.

"Father John," Drake interrupted.

"How… how did you know my name?" Father John asked.

"I know your name from a dream I had," Drake started. "I knew you were sitting there when we first waked in."

"We?"

"Yeah, me and my friend," Drake said as he pointed to the phoenix still in the doorway, "his name is Zack," Drake introduced them. Zack transformed back into a silver wolf.

"Oh my, a Seî. I have only read about them!" Father John shouted with delight as he tried to hugged Zack.

"What my parents wouldn't give to see this…" Drake started to say when he remembered the very end of his dream. "My parents!" Drake shouted in a very serious and concerned tone as he darted out of the room. While Drake rushed through the forest, tears started building up. As soon as he hit the field, Drake took off as fast as he could, hoping everything would be fine.

Chapter Four:

It Begins With A Flame

Tears were flowing down Drake's face as he stood in front of his home, watching it burn before his eyes. A few moments before, Drake was running through his city, trying to find his parents. They must have gotten out before the fire but where were they?

"Hello?" Drake shouted. "Is anyone there?" There was no response. The only sound he heard was the fire burning behind him. Drake started to freak out when Zack came running up to him. "Zack? How did you find me?" Drake asked. "Your scent," Zack replied. In the distance he saw a girl, around his age, covered in blood, bruises, and torn clothes standing in front of a flaming building. "Hello?" Drake shouted at her. "Hey, can you hear me?" She just stood there. He started walking towards her and when he was about three-fourths of the way there, the girl turned, looked at him, and took off running. "Wait!" Drake shouted as he took off after the girl. She ran to the end of the street and turned. Drake ran as fast as he could, and when he got to the end of the street, he couldn't find her. Suddenly, he spotted the same girl, standing in front of a collapsed housing building, staring at him. He took off running towards her again and like last time, when he got close, the girl took off running again.

This routine continued for several blocks, and soon Drake was catching his breath in front of the library. Drake looked around and saw the girl at the top of the stairs, in front of the entrance to the library. As soon as he spotted her, she went running inside. After catching his breath, he entered the library with caution. While inside, everything seemed normal, except for the fact that no one was around and partially destroyed. As Drake walked through the library, he noticed the Tёrcerlin symbol scattered everywhere. Drake suddenly remembered the rest of his "nightmare." Drake walked up to an old book and as soon as he was directly in front of the book, the Tёrcerlin symbol that was on the spine started to glow. Drake grabbed the book but instead of sitting down to read it, he left the library. Drake made his way through the city to the hole in the outer wall. He walked up to the hole. Just before he entered it, he remembered he had completely forgotten Zack back at the library.

"Zack!" Drake called out to him. It rang throughout the city. Shortly, Zack was in Drake's view, heading right for him. Once he got there, the two entered the forest together. Zack and Drake spent hours wandering the forest. Finally, Zack got curious.

"So where are we going and what's that in your hand?"

"Oh this?" Drake asked as he held the book up for Zack to see. "This is called a book and I'm looking for the doorway to speak to Father John again."

"Well why didn't you say so," Zack replied. He stopped, sat, and started wagging his tale. "I know how you get there!"

"Really? How?"

"Don't seek with your eyes. Seek with your heart."

"What is that supposed to mean?"

"That's how you find the Lost Library."

"Oh that's nonsense!" Drake said with a chuckle. "Come on." So for the rest of the day, Drake and Zack looked for the doorway but had no luck. Nighttime soon fell and Drake and Zack were eating a tasty zerminien Zack caught with no effort. Later that night, Drake took a walk alone. He made sure Zack wasn't going to wake up first. Before he knew it, he was far enough from the campsite. "Don't seek with your eyes. Seek with your heart." Drake thought about this phrase but just couldn't figure it out. He took a break for a moment.

"I give up," Drake said and started heading back to the campsite when something caught his attention. It was a stone doorway. "Don't seek with your eyes. Seek with your heart." Drake finally understood what it meant. He hurried over to it. After touching the doorway like last time, Drake embraced for searing pain. When Drake slowly opened his eyes, the top of his hand was glowing. The burn marks were back but there was no pain; only light. It was at that moment while taking a good look at the Tërcerlin glowing on his hand that

Drake accepted the fact that he is 'The Chosen One'. He held up his hand to the stone doorway and a door appeared. Drake looked around to make sure he was still alone then entered the door. Drake walked into the Lost Library where Father John was putting away some old books and scrolls.

"I see you came back," Father John paused, "Chosen One." Drake walked up to him and handed him the book from the Jewel City library. "Well hello to you too," he told Drake.

"I'm sorry father. Good even….," Drake started to say.

"You found the Book of Mirrors I see," Father John interrupted. The two walked over to a table.

"I had a dream about this book," Drake said as they sat down.

"You dreamt about more than this book, didn't you?" Father John asked.

"How did you know?"

"You have a special gift called Sitiluo."

"What's Sitiluo?"

"Sitiluo is the ability to see into the future."

"Sweet!"

"Now hold on, there's more. Only one person every one-hundred years is gifted with this power but this power is uncontrollable."

"What do you mean uncontrollable?"

"Well your visions, as they are called, will come to you asleep or wide awake. Also, the visions can be about anyone or anywhere, but most of the time, you'll get visions of your own future." He paused a moment, "wait, why *DO* you have the Book of Mirrors?"

"I think something very bad is happening," Drake said as he opened the book. Then, just like in his vision, the two of them watched the city fall from the sky around them. The two fell into an almost paralyzed state of pure horror as they watched innocent people fall with the city. Finally, just like before, part of the city fell on Drake but this time, it fell on Father John too. The two opened their eyes and they were back in the Lost Library.

"Is that really happening?" Drake asked with a serious tone.

"I'm....I'm afraid so," Father John sadly responded. An eerie silence fell over the room. He slowly closed the book.

"Here," he said as he pushed the book in front of Drake, "keep this book safe."

"Okay?" Drake said confused. Father John got up and started to gather some things. "What are you doing?" Drake asked.

"Preparing for our journey," Father John replied.

"Journey?"

"We are going to where that city just fell."

"But what about my family and friends? Everyone from my city has gone missing." Father John paused from his task.

"I was afraid you would mention this," he said slowly and quietly.

"Mention what?" Drake asked. Father John walked back over to Drake.

"Follow me," he said. Drake got up and followed Father John over to a bookshelf. He grabbed an old scroll and handed it to Drake. "Hold this please," he asked. Drake took the scroll. Father John reached into the spot where the scroll was; as far back as he could. After a few seconds, a *click* sound came from behind the bookshelf. Father John pulled his hand out, went to the end of the bookshelf and pulled out another scroll, handing it to Drake. Just like before, he stuck his hand into the spot where the scroll was. Another *click* sound.

Father John grabbed both scrolls from Drake and placed them back where they were. Finally, he walked to a different bookshelf and pulled one side open, reveling a secret staircase. Father John hurried down the stairs, with Drake right behind him. As the two started down the stairs, the bookshelf closed behind them. Drake was in pure awe when he got to the bottom of the staircase. He was now truly in the Lost Library. Books and scrolls were everywhere; thousands and thousands of them. "Here," Father John said as he walked over to a book, pulled it out, and handed it to Drake.

"What's this?" he asked.

"Open it." Drake hesitated for a moment then opened the cover. "Michael Cashner," it stated.

"Who is this guy?" Drake asked as he started skimming through the book, hoping Father John would tell him.

"Mr. Cashner was one of the worst criminals alive. He would kidnap people in the dead of night and torture them in horrifying ways until they died right in front of him. He was a very ruthless killer."

"What happened to him?" Drake asked, actually interested.

"No one really knows. The Hieds finally found his location but when they got there, no one was to be found except for the hundreds of bodies left to rot away."

"When was this?" Drake was really interested now.

Father John noticed the interest glowing from Drake and started laughing, "Oh that was years ago."

"So they never caught him, did they?" Drake asked as he closed the book and handed it back to Father John.

"No," Father John replied as he put the book away and grabbed another. He handed Drake the new book, "This is who is causing all the trouble right now." Drake opened the cover, "Christopher Anders. This is the guy from the most wanted list," Drake recognized the name from the news the other day.

"That's correct, and I believe he had something to do with that city falling."

"So let's go find him and turn him in," Drake stated eagerly.

"Actually, we should go to where the city fell. There might be survivors that need our help."

"Yeah, you're right. But how do we get there?" Just as Father John was about to speak, the library shook for a few seconds. "What the….," Drake started to ask but there was another shake. This one lasted a bit longer.

"Quick! Go see what's happening," Father John demanded as he started to quickly grab some items. Without hesitation, Drake went running upstairs. While heading up, the ground shook harder. Drake finally made his way outside. Everything looked normal except for a light red color to the north, almost like city lights. Drake took off running towards the lighted sky. The ground kept shaking, worse and worse as he kept running. Drake got to the very edge of the forest and froze. Hundreds of armed Hieds were surrounding the outer wall to his city but that wasn't what stopped Drake. His beloved city was halfway on fire with bombs going off inside the city. Screams from inside pierced the silence around him. Crying, Drake knew he couldn't move or someone might shoot him so all he could do was watch his entire life change before his eyes.

Chapter Five:

Truth Be Told

Drake opened his eyes wide and shot up. He looked around and found himself inside a tent. Drake noticed his shoes were by the opening. He put them on and headed out of the tent. Father John was making what looked like stew over a fire and Zack was putting more wood on the fire with his teeth. Drake looked up at the sky; crystal clear. He stood there, remembering what happened last night. He was just about to dart towards his home when everything went black and Drake fell to the ground, unconscious.

"Good morning Drake," Father John said as he waved Drake over to him.

"Morning," Drake replied.

"Here, eat this. You'll need as much energy for this journey as you can get," Father John stated as he handed Drake a bowl of the stew he had made. Without hesitation, Drake took the bowl and started eating. Beef, potatoes, onions, and a few berries was all Drake could taste as he scarfed down the bowl. "Well, I'm glad to see that my cooking is delicious."

"That it is!" Drake said as he handed the bowl back, "what is it?"

"It's called Digelo. Would you like some more?"

"Yes please!"

"Well help yourself." Drake filled his bowl almost to the brim. The taste was actually an off sweet taste but Drake didn't care. It was food and boy, was Drake hungry. After eating, Drake helped clean everything up and soon, the three of them were on their way.

"What um," Drake paused, "what happened last night?"

"Whatever do you mean?" Father John asked, knowing the answer anyway.

"What happened after I saw my home on fire? Why were there hieds in the front of the city's outer wall? What about my parents? And Kim?"

"Slow down, slow down." Father John started from the beginning after taking a deep sigh," About a week ago, I had a vision of your parents being….," he stopped walking, "being taken by a couple of armed hied guards. They took them somewhere; I'm not sure where but it wasn't…."

"Where are they now? Why did they go after my parents?" Drake interrupted.

"Do you know it's very rude to interrupt people?"

"Sorry," Drake apologized.

"Thank you. The next day, I had a vision of you meeting me for the first time. I instantly knew you and your parents were in danger so when you started off on your trip with your friend Kim, I visited your parents and warned them. They agreed to leave the city and head towards Crystral. There, they would be safe in open water. As I was leaving the city to prepare for our encounter, I ran into your friend Kim, crying and freaking out about you. I convinced her to go home, pack her personals, and leave with your parents. Then, we met." He ended and started walking again, with Zack following. Drake stood there for a moment soaking up the information.

"So they will be okay?" Drake asked as he quickly caught up to Father John and Zack.

"Yes Drake, I promise," Father John said with reassurance.

"Wait!" Drake stopped.

"What?" thought Zack as Father John and himself stopped as well.

"What happened last night though? All I remember was seeing those armed hieds around the city as well as the city on fire and were those bombs going off inside the city?" Drake asked almost angrily.

"I put a spell on you that instantly put you to sleep," Father John said.

"What? Why?"

"You were about to run towards armed men in the middle of the night. They are trained to kill without hesitation when ordered and by the look of things last night," he paused, looking at Drake to finish his sentence.

"I wouldn't be here right now?" Drake slowly asked.

"Correct."

"Wow. Thank you but what was going on?"

"Christopher Anders knows about 'The Chosen One'. Somehow, he knew that he or she was living in your city; Jewel City. He blew a hole in the city's outer wall and that's how he got in as well as how you got out."

"What about the hieds?"

"I'm unsure about that one, but I'll explain more once we get to where we are needed most." Father John took off walking again, shortly followed by Drake and Zack. Before they knew it, they were on a dirt road, heading in the opposite direction of the setting sun. Drake caught himself taking in the nature around him, not realizing the fork in the road up ahead. Father John stopped and looked at the sign posted next to the fork; to the North was Deller's Pass, to the East was Hill Lands, and to the West (behind them) was Dersi Forest and Jewel City.

"This way," he said as he pointed at the sign that read Hill Lands.

"Okay," replied Drake as the three continued walking. The sun soon set and camp was set up a little ways off the road. Usually, Drake was beyond excited for Digelo but there was so much going on so fast that Drake simply acted like he was excited. After dinner, Drake decided to turn in early, or so he told Zack and Father John. While inside his tent, Drake started thinking about his mother and father. He was so worried about them. Drake needed to get his mind off of things. He was extremely tired and just wanted to sleep. He closed his eyes and listened to the sounds and noises around him. First, he heard Father John putting the fire out and going to bed. He tried harder to hear outside the general area. Slithering sounds were all the animal noises he could hear while sounds of waves crashing against a shoreline seemed close.

The sounds and noises slowly put Drake to sleep; just as he was hoping it would.

The next morning, after eating, packing up camp, and getting back on the road, they came to the beginning of the Hill Lands.

"Now this is where our day truly begins," Father John chuckled as he started up the first hill. Drake and Zack just looked confusedly at each other and followed behind.

Hill after hill was all the three could see as the day moved on, but that evening, things got ugly. The three were at the bottom of a large hill when they noticed the temperature was changing.

"It feels like a storm is brewing ahead," Father John predicted.

"Yeah, let's go check it out," Drake said, a bit curious. Drake had never left Jewel City before. The law had always forbidden it. This could have been Drake's only chance to see as much as he could and to watch a storm come in from far away was definitely on Drake's list of things to see. He took off running up the hill.

"Now wait for me!" Father John shouted as he tried to catch up with Drake. Zack was right behind. Once the other two finally reached the top of the hill and after only shortly regaining their breath back, the three stood there looking out at the Hill Lands. Up ahead, destroyed and still on fire remained the once mighty floating city of Azel.

Chapter Six:

It's Ancient History

Drake couldn't move; neither could Father John or Zack. Chaos seemed endless across the now fallen city, but why did this city fall to begin with? Cries of loss and pain rang through the hills as an eerie chill slowly fell as the storm headed their way.

"Hurry. We need to help as many people as we can before the storm gets here and makes things worse," said Father John as he snapped out of his shock and started to hurry down the hill towards what looked like people below. Drake turned towards Zack and nodded in agreement and started down the hill. Zack took off above the two below, looking out for danger.

"Help! Please help us!" Drake heard a lady yell from in front of them.

"Hurry!" Drake shouted as he took off running as fast as he could down the hill.

"Please sir! Please help us!" the lady asked Drake as he ran up to her. He looked at the lady; some bruises, ripped and burned clothes, and blood scattered all over her. There were a few more men and women, as well as some children. Drake looked over at the children and absolute pure fear was on every child's face. Father John shortly joined Drake and Zack just kept an eye above them.

"What happened?" Father John asked the lady.

"Honestly, I don't know. One moment, we were all fine, enjoying a beautiful day. The next thing we knew, the city was falling apart and out of the sky. We are all that survived without major harm."

"How many are behind?"

"Eight or nine."

"How many were there before this happened?" Drake asked. The lady and the rest of the people bowed their heads.

"Over a thousand of us once lived in Azel," she said as she raised her head.

"Well, let's get to it then," Father John said to cut the painful conversation. "Drake, go ahead to the site and help in any way. I'll stay here and set up a campsite until we can get help. Ma'am, I need a few of you who can, to go with my friend here back to the wounded and try to bring them here. The rest of you will help me set up and help the wounded." Father John said.

"Yes Father," Drake said.

"Okay," the lady agreed. "I'm Jane, Jane Florence."

"Father John Hae, pleasure to help," Father John introduced himself.

"And I'm Drake Shaw," Drake introduced himself as well.

"Thank you Father John and Drake! Thank you so much for your help!" Jane said with some delight. After dividing the two teams up, Drake, Jane, and their crew headed back for the wounded while Father John and his crew started camp.

By the time Drake and his crew got back with the first round of wounded and injured, the camp was all set up and functional. There was a place for surgery, food, and rest. On Drake's second round, the storm finally arrived and the rain fell and fell. On the final round, it was still raining and night was coming.

"You ready Drake?" Jane asked.

"I want to walk around real quick, if that's okay."

"Sure, but don't be gone too long." Drake looking off, looking and hoping for at least one or two more survivors left. He was having no luck at all when he heard a small noise. He stopped and listened closely. It sounded like knocking. Drake listened closer, following the noise. It definitely was knocking.

"Hello? Hello? Is anyone there?" Drake shouted.

"Hello! Over here!" he heard a man shout from somewhere in the rubble around him.

"Keep shouting sir so I can find you," Drake shouted.

"My name is Father Izea and I am grateful that you are for looking for me...." As Father Izea talked, Drake listened and shortly found him.

"Alright, Father Izee? I need you to push as hard as you can when I count to three, okay?" Drake said loudly as he positioned himself to try to lift the stone that was trapping the man.

"Okay," Father Izea shouted.

"One….two….three!" As Father Izea pushed from the inside, Drake lifted the sides up. The stone slowly lifted higher and higher until Drake lifted it high enough to tip it completely over, mostly by himself. Father Izea slowly came up from a small hole that was made by the debris.

"It's Father Izea and thank you young one for saving my life."

"Oh, it's nothing and I apologize for mispronouncing your name. I'm Drake Shaw." Drake stuck his hand out to shake Father Izea's hand. As their hands met, Father Izea shouted as pain expanded from his shoulder outwards.

"You're hurt!" Drake immediately let go and grabbed a rag from his back pocket that was given to him by Jane and made a sling for Father Izea.

"Thank you Drake," he said.

"You're welcome but try not to move it," Drake warned. Not really wanting to listen to a kid, Father Izea agreed and followed Drake. As the two walked around the rubble, they heard a small noise. It sounded like falling rubble. They quickly looked around and saw a man trying to push the rubble off of his feet.

"King Evergreen!" shouted Father Izea as he ran up to the man.

"King?" Drake asked as he followed Father Izea.

"My lord, are you alright?" Father Izea asked as he helped try to push off the large amount of rubble that was crushing his feet. Drake helped but it was no use; the rubble was too heavy.

"Father....," King Evergreen started off.

"Yes my lord?"

"I....I don't have much time," he said. King Evergreen was in searing pain.

"Just hold on my lord. We will go get help."

"There's no time....," he paused, "find my son and tell him that it is time. He needs to fine 'The Chosen One' and assist him in anyway. If he fails, then all hope.... all hope will be lost." There was silence as King Evergreen was taking his last breaths. "You, child. Come closer." Drake got close. King Evergreen grabbed his hands. "Help my friend here to safety please."

"Of course my lord," Drake responded. He backed up and Father Izea knelt next to the dying king, nearly shoving Drake into the rubble. He whispers something into Father Izea's ear. He nodded.

"I....I....," King Evergreen started to say but never finished. The two stood there for a moment of silence for the now dead king. Father Izea started crying. Drake wanted to comfort Father Izea but he realized that he wasn't comfortable around young "non-obedient" children. Father Izea wiped his tears and the two headed back to camp.

That night, Drake didn't see Father Izea or one of the older children at dinner. In fact, he hadn't noticed them at all since they got back to camp. Drake started to wonder what was going on. He walked around the edge of the camp when he heard talking.

"You sure we should do this Father?" a young boy, older than Drake by a few years said quietly.

"Yes, now hurry my prince," came Father Izea's voice. Immediately, Drake spotted the two hidden behind some rocks.

"Prince?" Drake said as he popped around the corner, startling the two.

"Yes, I'm Prince Evergreen," the young boy said.

"My prince," Father Izea started saying.

"It's alright Father," Prince Evergreen interrupted. "Look, I'm not safe here so Father Izea and I are leaving now. Do you understand?"

"Of course, my prince," Drake said as he bowed in respect.

"Thank you," he said as he held his hand out to shake Drakes. Drake extended his and as the two shook hands, the Tërcerlin on Drake's hand started glowing, nearly blinding the two. Just as Prince Evergreen and Drake let go, the glow quickly faded away. "Are....are you....are you 'The Chosen One'?" he asked in shock.

"Are you alright?" Drake asked as the prince nearly fell.

"Yeah, I'm alright."

"I'm 'The Chosen One', yes," Drake said after a sigh.

"He's the one Father Izea, the one I am destined to help," Prince Evergreen said as he started to take off his pack. He sat Drake down and started to explain everything.

"I'm sorry to interrupt you but what does that have to do with me?" Drake interrupted.

"How dare you interrupt his highness!" Father Izea snarled as he continued to stare Drake down.

"It's alright Father. He's fine," he told Father Izea calmly. He turned back to Drake and continued.

"It says that one day, Darkness will awaken again, spreading fear and pain. As the Darkness gets stronger, 'The Chosen One' will be revealed and will face the Darkness. You're 'The Chosen One' Drake. It's up to you to defeat this evil and bring peace to the universe again."

"What if I don't want to? What if I don't want to be 'The Chosen One' or save the universe?" Drake asked.

"It is destiny child," Father Izea said strongly. "It is destiny that made Prince Evergreen prince, it is destiny that made me a priest, and it is destiny that made you 'The Chosen One'. That's the way of life."

"Ah Drake, there you are," said Father John as he slowly made his way around the rocks.

"Oh hey. Sorry, I was just chatting with some friends," Drake said a bit nervously.

"Friends huh? Well that's good," he replied.

"Father….Father John?" Father Izea asked.

"Father Izea? Is…. is that you?" Father John and Father Izea hugged each other then started talking to each other as they left the other two alone.

"Here, take this," Prince Evergreen said as he handed Drake a scroll. "This scroll is the entire history of the universe. All of your questions will be answered there." He picked his things up. "Good luck…. we are all counting on you Drake," he said as he patted Drake on the shoulder and walked away. Drake took a deep sigh and opened the scroll, unsure of what to expect.

Nothing. He opened it more. Still nothing. There was nothing on the scroll. No letters. No numbers. Not even a symbol of any kind. The prince must have been playing a trick on him but later that night, he found out it wasn't a trick.

As Drake laid on his coe, he kept opening and closing the scroll but couldn't find anything.

"Stupid scroll," he whispered as he threw the scroll at his shoes on the ground. The scroll hit the shoes and opened up, but Drake was too tired to get up and put it away. He just rolled over and went to sleep. As Drake started to drift off to sleep, words in an ancient text slowly appeared on the scroll. Then, the words changed from a black ink to a glowing blue. Gradually, the words floated off the scroll, bringing color and light with it, almost like a powerful sorcerer casting an enchantment. The words, colors, and light slowly drifted over Drake's head and into his ears, where it went into his brain to where his dream was starting, only but to force Drake to have a different dream; a dream of how the universe began.

Chapter Seven:
Knowing The Past

When time began, the cosmos created Light and Darkness, which had always coexisted with each other in peace and harmony. Light brought light, joy, and life while Darkness brought darkness, pain, and death. Light and Darkness together created the universe. When it was completed, two great and powerful beings appeared, Lord Taoî and Queen Evë. Lord Taoî picked the title of Master of Darkness, which Queen Evë choose the title of Guardian of Light. As the two beings parted ways, their reign scattered across the universe. Soon, species were choosing sides and perfect harmony was formed…. until The Great War began.

It all started with the Oîrkz on their home planet Farî. As Lord Taoî's favorite species, he saw a lot of darkness within the species that he helped them build the Murcurî Cannon. While the power supply of Cörsîoa Ores was deep within Farî, the Murcurî Cannon became useless, that is until one oîrk found a secret tunnel leading to a huge Cörsîoa Ore deposit. Smoke started spewing from the factories around the base of the Murcurî Cannon which raised concern with Queen Evë. Cloaked with dark magic, Queen Evë couldn't see what was exactly going on inside. Then it stopped, just as it started. Nothing happened though; no fire, no explosion, no anything.

The Great War began when King Orzoîrk (under direct orders from Lord Taoî) fired the Murcurî Cannon. The fire came with no warning. The target was Zoigë, Queen Evë's favorite and most valuable planet.

Zoigë was at the center of the universe, and when Zoigë choose Queen Evë, Light gave her three stones. Each stone was made from each sun, capturing light. The three stones where placed on Zoigë and when the three met, they created a light so powerful that it kept Darkness to the far reaches of the universe. Beyond furious, Lord Taoî wanted revenge. When the Oîrkz came up with the Murcurî Cannon idea, Lord Taoî saw this as a window of opportunity and seized it.

A ball of cosmic energy hit the heart of Zoigë, Mogämoir. Mogämoir was where the three stones were placed. As the entire planet exploded, light faded a bit across the universe. Queen Evë did not have the power of rebirth so she was forced to watch millions of pieces of her once beloved planet fly across the universe and beyond. Still wanting revenge, Lord Taoî prepared for his next target and The Great War truly began.

After the destruction of Zoigë, conflict started on Bosoî. Bosolîm brother's turned against each other causing wars and death. Some wanted to serve the Light while others held to Darkness. Parts of Bosoî became non-habitable, causing even more wars to occur. Soon, the entire planet was in chaos and was heading towards total destruction.

Meanwhile, on Brigdertîl, trouble started stirring. A powerful sorcerer finally created a space bridge, but there was only enough power to reach its neighboring planet Möwatei. He discovered that the entire planet was covered with water except for one island where most of the Winäras species lived. The Brîgi's were a dying race and needed something more stable to live on because several massive earthquakes had hit Brigdertîl and more were soon to come. The Brîgi thought if they could travel and live on Möwatei, their species might just survive but they knew that the Winäras wouldn't go down without a fight so they sent the sorcerer through the space bridge to exterminate the

Winäras. He cast a spell and raised the waters on Möwatei, flooding the only piece of land and all who lived on it. After the flooding, one survivor remained. To protect herself, she contained her soul into a glass sphere and was shot out into space, hoping maybe one day, her species would live on.

While Möwatei was being flooded, Azermös's conflict started with its three moons. The three moons would soon align as one and whoever wields the Staff of Healing Prayers would have complete control of the planet. Empress Aäi held the staff, knowing that Darkness would try and take it. Empress Aäi's highest knight, Sir Emersî grew jealous of her and sided with Darkness. One night, he snuck into Empress Aäi's chambers and stole the staff. Soon after, war started infesting the entire planet as the three moons got closer and closer. The final battle took place on the day of the alignment. War had consumed the planet and the last place still standing was the empress' palace. As the three moons started to align, Sir Emersî and Empress Aäi clashed swords. With a final blow, Sir Emersî was finally defeated. Empress Aäi grabbed the staff just as the three moons aligned as one and brought Light to Azermös. After the alignment, Empress Aäi and the remaining Jäpiz worked together to start restoring Azermös to its once bright and shining world.

The Great War came to a halt. After the marvelous winning on Azermös, Queen Evë was ready for Lord Taoî's next move but nothing happened. Was he finally giving up? Something big was happening and Queen Evë was determined to find out what it was and stop it for good. Lord Taoî stayed hidden in the shadows, smiling for his next move would change the war and give him a huge advantage. When the universe was created, two planets had enough gravity to pull each other close enough to be one another's moon. Each planet became identical to each other. So the "two planets" were named Trîmerce but the species of Dîomi Elves thrived on only one planet. With Lord Taoî's help, he persuaded the Dîomi Elves to build a portal strong enough to open on the other planet. In cooperation, the Dîomi Elves swore their allegiance in him and to Darkness itself. Immediate work began on the Darî Portal and just like that, it caught Queen Evë's attention right away. Lord Taoî knew she would go for the bait and quickly started on his actual plan.

On the far side of Farî, deep within the Forbidden Mountains laid an untouched valley of Cörsîoa Ores. Secret underground tunnels were made and the ores were taken to the Murcurî Cannon. Meanwhile on Trîmerce, the portal was nearly complete but Lord Taoî needed more time so he changed the blueprints to the portal. Now, in order to activate it, the Dîomi Elves needed a tear from the Shyzrl, which would also permanently keep the portal open. The Shyzrl was a horrifying beast that terrorized the Dîomi Elves once a year, killing almost half their population, destroying everything in its path, having no remorse whatsoever. As many elves gathered together to retrieve the tear, they decided to kill this foul beast once and for all. The battle was gruesome and only one elf survived, but the tear was retrieved and the beast was slayed. The Shyzrl's death provided enough time for Lord Taoî and King Orzoîrk. Just as the portal was completed and operational, the Murcurî Cannon was ready for firing. Queen Evë was still distracted by the traveling of planets on Trîmerce, giving Lord Taoî the chance to change the cannon's target. Just as the Murcurî Cannon was in place, Queen Evë sensed a greater danger.

By time she figured out what Lord Taoî was really up to, it was too late. A ball of cosmic energy shot out of the cannon and headed for its destination; Sun Ea.

Lord Taoî's grin quickly vanished off his face as he watched the ball fly right past the sun. King Orzoîrk had angled the cannon too far and now, the ball was headed towards Cruz. Cruz was an unknown planet to both Lord Taoî and Queen Evë. With a dense and thick fog surrounding the planet and rings of rocks that were constantly moving around the planet, the two never really bothered exploring it. The ball of energy barely missed a ring of rocks at it headed towards the mysterious planet and just like that, it disappeared into the fog. Moments past, then without any warning, the entire planet exploded. Lord Taoî wasn't celebrating though. It turned out, Cruz was a planet filled with so much Cörsîoa Ores that when the ball of cosmic energy struck the planet, it became a nuclear explosion. As the explosion carried across the universe, every planet, moon, and sun instantly exploded. Queen Evë only had but a few seconds to do something to prevent Darkness from winning. She instantly came up with enough power to protect Sun Ti and Evë, a planet she visited quite often. She chose these two because it was the farthest planet and sun from the oncoming explosion.

As the nuclear explosion hit the sun and Evë, nothing happened to it, as though they were untouched. Queen Evë was so weak from protecting the sun and planet, she barely had enough power to teleport herself into the Realm of Light, a realm separated between time and space. Lord Taoî, on the other hand, had a worse fate. He wasn't going to flee to the Realm of Darkness. He was going to face this explosion and as it hit him, the explosion was so powerful that it tore his soul into five artifacts. As soon as the explosion had settled, the protection spell slowly dissipated over the sun and Evë. The five artifacts somehow floated right towards the remaining planet and crashed in different locations across it.

Deep within the Realm of Light, Queen Evë was still very weak. She used the realms powers to create a symbol to bring Light back into the universe and entrusted it to one person who would have enough courage and heart to face Darkness itself. That person would be called 'The Chosen One' and it would be up to him or her to defeat the forces of Darkness and restore balance to the universe.

Chapter Eight:

After The War

After the Great War, Queen Evë was beginning her rest in the Realm of Light, which didn't take much time at all. Unfortunately, she did not have enough power to leave the Realm of Light yet.

"Saving one small pathetic planet won't stop me from winning," came Lord Taoî's voice from out of nowhere. Immediately, Queen Evë looked for the Master of Darkness but there was no sign of him.

"You may not have been defeated, but you are permanently trapped," Queen Evë said.

"Permanently?" Lord Taoî started chuckling, "I can never be permanently trapped. See, as long as there is Darkness, there will be at least one who will follow it." Queen Evë looked worried.

"Uswa may, ta kata wa," she started chanting, "uswa may, ta kata wa." Lord Taoî stopped chuckling. "Uswa may, ta kata wa." She was casting a spell on the five artifacts for whoever reunites them and released Lord Taoî will begin to suffer a fate worse than death and only one spell, which Queen Evë knew could cure him or her.

"Stop it!" shouted Lord Taoî for every time she spoke that phrase, he could feel his powers getting weaker.

"Uswa may, ta kata wa," Queen Evë continued chanting, "uswa may, ta kata wa." Then silence, from both parties.

"Your time will come!" Lord Taoî screeched, echoing throughout the realm. Queen Evë waited for another response but nothing. On the ground, she drew the Tërcerlin symbol. As soon as she completed it, a portal like mirror appeared within the largest circle's walls. It was planet Evë. She then sat down and watched, waiting for the right time to appear once again.

Chapter Nine:

A Dark Plan

He closed the lid, locked it, and placed the black box next to him. He took the key and chain and placed it around his neck. The two soldiers across from him didn't say a word.

"This box is to never leave this building unless I, myself say so. Is that understood?" Mr. Anders asked as he stood up and grabbed the box.

"Sir yes sir!" shouted the men simultaneously.

"Good." The soldiers followed Mr. Anders into an empty room except for a stone stand in the center of the room. He placed the box in the center of the stand and a light appeared directly above the box, shining only on the box. The three then exited the room. The two soldiers stood guard outside the room as Mr. Anders left the building. He walked along a rocky path, heading towards Mount Fire. The closer he got, the hotter it got.

Up ahead was a temple on the side of the mountain. Once inside, Mr. Anders walked to the most sacred room. It was almost pitch black and in a far corner, a shadow like figure sat. Mr. Anders immediately knelt before the figure.

"Well?" the figure spoke.

"I retrieved what you have asked for, your lordship," Mr. Anders replied.

"You have done quite well Mr. Anders. I'm impressed."

"Thank you, your lordship."

"I have another task, if you're up for it."

"Of course, your lordship." stated Mr. Anders as he got up. The figure started to move. It stood up and walked towards Mr. Anders but stopped a few inches before the only light in the room.

"I want you to travel to the Rocky Region to the city of Tii. There, a priest named Father Brai has some valuable information I require. Bring him to me."

"I shall teleport there immediately!" assured Mr. Anders.

"No!" demanded the figure. "Father Brai can detect dark magic and would know you were coming. Take the eglîmos. They are best known for their excellent rock climbing skills."

"As you wish, my lordship," accepted Mr. Anders. The figure returned to sitting.

"Begone," the figure said. Mr. Anders rushed out of the room. He hurried back to Moonshiar and the moment he got there, he gathered men and supplies. After the eglîmos were saddled up and after the men were fed, they began their two day journey to Tii.

As the sun started to rise, Drake, Zack, and Father John were already up and on their way. As the sun continued to rise over the Hill Lands, the journey seemed to get longer and longer as they climbed hill after hill.

"This is taking forever," Drake finally said as he stopped on top of a hill to rest.

"Good idea Drake," Father John said as he stopped, "let's rest for a bit." Zack flew down and transformed from a blue-tail bird into a silver wolf.

"Hey Zack? Why do you turn into a silver wolf all the time?" Drake asked.

"Well, it's my favorite!" Zack thought delightfully. After resting, the three continued on. It was about mid-afternoon when they came to a fork in the road. To the left was Deller's Pass and the Rocky Region, to the right was Lake Miir and the Eastern Mountains, in front of them was the Hedia Mountains and Moonshiar, and behind them was the Hill Lands, the Northern Plains, and Jewel City. They took the left and continued. Slowly, the Rocky Region came into view. Just as the sun was setting, they came to the base of the Rocky Region. Drake looked around but all he could see was the mountains.

"Let us set up camp here for the night," Father John said. Drake agreed and soon, the camp was up and nighttime had fallen. When everyone turned in that night, Drake couldn't seem to get to sleep. As the night grew on, he slowly started to drift away when a faint noise immediately woke him up. Drake got dressed and headed outside. The noise of getting out of his tent woke up Father John and Zack.

"What's going on?" Father John asked as he came out of his tent.

"I don't know but I heard something," Drake replied as he started off in the direction they came from.

"It was probably a wild creature," Father John assured.

"Maybe, but something doesn't feel right either."

"Something doesn't feel right?"

"How can you tell?" Zack asked.

"I don't know. It feels dark....," Drake paused, "dark and evil." This really caught Father John's attention. "There," Drake said as he pointed to a faint light in the distance. As the light got closer, more lights appeared.

"It looks like a caravan," Father John said, "There's nothing to worry about." But Drake still knew something wasn't right.

117

"Hey! Over here!" shouted Father John.

"What are you doing?" Drake immediately cut him off.

"Letting them know we are here."

"Why? I don't think it's a good idea."

"Nonsense," Father John said, "Everything will be alright."

"Drake's right. It's not a good idea," Zack thought.

"We're over here!" shouted Father John, completely ignoring Zack. The lights stopped for a moment then started heading towards the three at a fast pace. Whatever those lights were, they were coming right at them. Father John kept hollering while Drake grabbed his things. Him and Zack took off up one of the mountain sides. They came to a safe spot and watched as the lights came to their camp below. There were about ten or eleven men on eglîmos that circled Father John. Drake and Zack were too far away to hear what was going on. A man got off his eglîmo and walked up to Father John. Shortly afterwards, the man drew a sword and right into Father John it went. He dropped to his knees. The man whispered something to Father John then pulled his sword out. Just as the tip came out, Father John fell over and died.

"No!" screamed Drake as he stood up with tears rushing down his face. The men looked at the direction Drake and Zack were hiding and took off towards them. The two took off running into the mountains. This was Drake's first deadly chase because he knew if he was caught, that would be the end of him.

Chapter Ten:

Into The Mountains

The chase had just begun and Drake was already out of breath. The men broke apart, looking for Drake and Zack who got separated at the beginning of the chase. One of the men spotted Drake and took off towards him. Drake started climbing faster when he accidentally slipped and fell. Before Drake could even get up, the man was right on top of him with his sword drawn and pointed right at Drake's throat. The man was about to swing when he suddenly stopped. The man noticed the Tërcerlin symbol on Drake's hand. Out of nowhere, Zack came charging in as an eglîmo. He ran right into the man, causing him to go flying.

"Quick! Get on!" thought Zack. Without any hesitation, Drake quickly got up and hopped onto

Zack's back. Zack took off, continuing to climb further into the Rocky Region.

The other men quickly came to aid their fallen comrade.

"After them you morons!" he shouted as he got himself up. The men took off towards Drake and Zack, followed by the man who got up. It turned out to be the leader of the group, Mr. Anders. As the men kept getting closer and closer to the two, the closer they were getting to Tii without even realizing it. As the two reached a ridge, they noticed lights to a town ahead. As they took off towards the town, the men were right on their tail. As the chase got closer to the town, a siren started going off. Dozens of archers appeared in front of the town, aimed right at the chase. Then, they fired. Drake and Zack braced themselves for the arrows but nothing happened. The archers were aiming at the men behind them, and only because of their lights. Drake and Zack didn't have anything to give them away so they blended in with the nighttime. The men were struck by the arrows but unfortunately, Drake and Zack couldn't stop. Out of nowhere, the two surprised the archers by accidentally running into them. Drake went flying when Zack ran into three archers. He flew until he hit a house, instantly becoming unconscious.

In the mountains just outside Tii, Mr. Anders slowly walked to where his men were. Some were killed and others were injured by the arrows.

"We got ambushed sir," a soldier started to speak, "There is only a few of us who survived." Without any hesitation, Mr. Anders beheaded the soldier.

"Does anyone else have anything to say?" The leader said in the deadliest tone. No one said a word. "That's what I thought," he paused, "Captain Ric." One of the soldiers hurried over to him. "Is the cargo safe?"

"Yes Mr. Anders sir," the captain said.

"Excellent," Mr. Anders said with a smile on his face as he stared at the city below.

As the sunlight slowly crept up to his eyes, it caused Drake to wake up. After adjusting his eyes, he looked around and realized he was in a bed inside somebody's home. He started to scratch his head when he realized his head was bandaged up. All of a sudden, the door opened and a head popped in.

"Oh, you're awake," a man said gladly then walked in. Drake scooted to the very end of the bed with fear in his eyes. "Oh no, I'm not going to hurt you," the man said as he approached the bed. "My name is Father Brai."

"Father Brai?" Drake asked with a bit of relief yet still cautious.

"Yes," he said. Instantly, Drake rushed into his arms and started crying. Father Brai knew Drake was the 'The Chosen One' by the Tërcerlin symbol on his hand. Drake was young and was almost killed. He let everything out because he knew Father Brai was a friend. Drake finally calmed down and started speaking.

"How long was I out?"

"A couple of days." Drake slowly rubbed his head when he realized something.

"I think you are in terrible danger Father Brai!" he said urgently.

"What are you talking about child?"

"The other night, those men you guys were shooting at were soldiers and they killed my friend Father John." Drake shot up from sitting on the bed. "I have a bad feeling not all of them are dead and for whatever reason, they were after Zack and....," he paused, "Where's Zack?"

"Zack?" Father Brai asked, "Who's Zack?"

"He's the, umm, creature I came crashing into town on," Drake seemed a bit worried.

"You mean that beast is your pet?"

"Not a pet, a friend." Father Brai started laughing.

"An eglîmo as your friend?" he asked sarcastically.

"He's not an eglaaa...aa..eglaa.... a whatever. He's a Seî." Drake started to get really worried. Immediately, Father Brai stopped laughing.

"A what?" he asked with a bit of worry in his tone.

"He's my friend, okay?" Drake was really starting to worry about where Zack was now.

"Oh dear!" Father Brai said in a very serious tone as he hurried over to a pile of clothes. "Quickly, put these on. We don't have much time," he said as he picked up the clothes and gave them to Drake.

"What's going on?" Drake asked.

"I'll explain on the way. Just hurry if you want to save your friend." Drake quickly changed and the two left the home towards the outskirts of town. They were almost to the outskirts when the attack happened.

It started off with a small rumble. To the West, Captain Ric came charging down into the town with about a hundred or so soldiers right behind him. Immediately, sirens started going off and people began freaking out. As the men got closer, archers appeared outside the city, as before. Unfortunately, there were too many soldiers. As they entered the town, they showed no mercy. They slayed anyone in their path; man, woman, and child. They set each building on fire and destroyed their town center.

"Quickly!" Father Brai said as he hurried into a building that hadn't been hit yet. Drake followed. Inside, Zack was tied up.

"Zack! Thank god!" Drake said as he quickly started to untie him.

"Hurry!" Father Brai said as he kept watch.

"Alright, we're ready," Drake said as he untied the last knot. Father Brai hurried over to the two and placed his hands on both Drake and Zack.

"Aba deloo a cky!" Father Brai chanted. There was a bright flash that blinded the two and just like that, they were gone. Drake opened his eyes to find they'd arrived in some kind of chamber. "We must hurry. We don't have much time before they find us."

"Before who finds us?" thought Zack.

"Remember those soldiers from the other night?" Drake asked. "Well they're back but this time, with a lot more men and they want everyone dead."

"Why?"

"I don't' know." While Drake and Zack were trying to figure out what was going on, Father Brai was gathering a few things. "Where are we anyway?"

"My chambers, under the city," Father Brai said while he grabbed the rest of the items he wanted. "Are you two ready?" he finally asked.

"Ready for what?" Drake asked.

"Space jumping. Just whatever you do, don't let go of me," Father Brai grabbed Drake's hand. Drake, who was already holding onto Zack only held on tighter. Father Brai held out a sphere. "Vinn Forest." As soon as he said their destination, the sphere started to glow green. "Hold on tight!" Father Brai shouted as he threw the sphere down in between the three. Green smoke appeared out of the sphere when it shattered, surrounding the three and teleporting them to their destination. As the smoke disappeared, so had Father Brai, Drake, and Zack. Moments later, the door to the chambers was barged in and several soldiers followed by Captain Ric and Mr. Anders entered the room.

"There's nobody here sir," one of the soldiers informed Mr. Anders. The two walked further into the room when Mr. Anders stepped on a piece of the broken sphere. He backed up and looked at it.

"Captain, bring me the cargo," he said. Captain Ric quickly handed him his bag. He searched through it until he found a small sphere. He bent down, picked up a sphere piece, and looked at it. A very small trace of green liquid was found on the piece.

"Meet me back at Moonshiar at once," he demanded, "I must take care of something…. personally." Everyone left the room except Mr. Anders.

"Soon we will be reunited again, old friend, he said as he looked at his sphere. "Vinn Forest," he said. The sphere started to glow green and he threw it on the ground below him. Just like the large sphere, it broke open and green smoke appeared, surrounding Mr. Anders. As the smoke cleared, he had disappeared.

Chapter Eleven:

Deep Within The Vinn Forest

Drake slowly opened his eyes to find it nighttime and deep within the forest.

"Welcome to Vinn Forest gentlemen," Father Brai said as he stretched himself out. Afterwards, he opened his bag up and pulled out a small black box. "Here," he said as he handed it to Drake, "open it."

"What is it?" Drake asked, looking confused.

"It's magical," Father Brai said with delight. Drake opened the box but there was nothing inside.

"Magical huh?" he said as he tossed the box. Once it hit the ground, it opened and started to shift and change. Before the three knew it, camp was set up right where he tossed it.

"Yes, magical," Father Brai said as he entered the camp. Drake felt stupid. After eating, Drake explained to Father Brai what Zack was and how he communicated with the two through Sitiluo. Father Brai has heard of Sitiluo but never thought he'd live to see the day where he finally would meet someone with this amazing gift. Zack transformed into several creatures for Father Brai, who seemed so delighted. Soon, the three headed to bed but for Drake, his night was just getting started. As Drake fell asleep, he started to dream.

It began as though he was waking up in daylight. As he got up, something didn't seem right. He looked around and noticed everything seemed brighter. He left his tent and looked for

Father Brai and Zack but neither one were to be seen.

"Hello?" Drake yelled but no response. "Is anyone there?" he yelled again and still no response. Suddenly, Drake heard a shuffling noise, almost like leaves moving. Drake looked around and around then spotted a girl peaking around a tree in the distance. He looked harder at the girl and noticed she was the same girl from the city, the one that led him to the library. Knowing this wasn't a coincidence, Drake started walking towards the girl. The girl then disappeared and peaked out again from a tree further back. Drake knew that she was drawing him away from camp but he continued anyway.

Soon, the girl appeared sitting on a rock in the middle of a small clearing. Drake slowly made his way to the edge of the clearing.

"Don't be afraid," the girl said but with a woman's voice.

"I'm not," Drake said confidently. The girl smiled, got up, and jumped off the rock towards Drake. While mid-air, the girl instantly grew into the most beautiful woman Drake had ever seen. Everything changed with the girl. Her clothes became an elegant dress and her hair became longer as well as changed colors. The woman landed a few feet in front of Drake. Her bright light complexion and white long hair mesmerized him so much, he walked up to her. "Who are you?" he asked.

"My name is Queen Evë, Guardian of Light," the woman spoke "you have done well my child."

"Thank you," he replied, not quite sure he knew what she meant.

"But there is much more ahead of you for you have only just begun your journey. Come."

"But why me?" Drake asked as he followed Queen Evë back into the forest.

"Well there are several reasons. One is you always seek adventure, even when there is no adventure to seek. Another is your eagerness to strive to get what you desire." She paused for a moment then stopped walking and turned towards Drake. "But most importantly, is the one where no matter the consequences, you will always put yourself and your own life in front of others, which means you have a very large heart with no fear," she said as she touched Drake's heart. Warmth radiated throughout his entire body. "Knowing that," she started, "you will always be unstoppable." Then, she turned around and continued walking. Drake followed right behind her, absorbing what she just said. Ancient ruins appeared ahead. The two stopped right in the middle of them.

"Where are we?" Drake asked, looking around.

"To be exact, we are in the Realm of Light. This particular location is the Stone Temple in the Vinn Forest, well what's left of the Stone Temple that is."

"Where is the Realm of Light?"

"Well you see....," she began, "before the universe was created, Light and Darkness lived peacefully in their own, separate realms. One day, the two met and a third realm of both Light and Darkness was created."

"Our universe," Drake said.

"That's correct. Somehow, when the universe was created, Lord Taoî and I were created too. We both chose sides and had access to our separate realms, keeping peace and harmony across the universe but Lord Taoî had other plans.

He thought he could control the third realm then take over the Realm of Light and rule forever."

"That's how The Great War started."

"That's right. After The Great War ended, the portals between realms closed, trapping myself in the Realm of Light."

"So how did I get here then?"

"You have special powers, allowing you to access the gates between the three realms."

"So how I am supposed to stop Darkness from taking over?"

"Somehow, Lord Taoî has contacted someone like you, but he serves Darkness. It's up to you to stop this man before he frees Lord Taoî."

"But how?"

"Lord Taoî's soul is trapped five artifacts: The Ruby of Gruîd Almighty, the Lost Soul of Möwatei, The Stones of Stones, The Elemental Orbs, and the Tërcerlin Stone. Together, they are known as the Ancient Five. If these artifacts were to be placed together by the wrong hands, Lord Taoî would be freed and would seek a revenge beyond revenges. Whoever this person that Lord Taoî has chosen, he already has three of the five artifacts. You must go and find the other two."

"I will," Drake assured her.

"There is a girl named Jessica McGee in your town. She will be able to help you find the last two artifacts."

"But how do I get there?" By this point in his journey, he couldn't tell North from South. He didn't even know where Vinn Forest was if he was looking for it on a map. Queen Evë walked up to a remaining wall and cast a spell on it. Instantly, the Tërcerlin symbol appeared at the top of the wall.

"This is a portal that leads directly to Jewel City. You must hurry though. The portal will not stay open for long."

"Okay."

"One more thing! Darkness is headed for you and your friends as we speak. Be careful Drake. If Darkness gets to Jessica before you do, there may be dire consequences."

"Will I ever see you again?"

"If fate allows it. Now go and no matter what Drake, be strong!" Instantly, everything went black.

Drake slowly opened his eyes and sat up. It was still nighttime. He looked around, only to find out he was still in his tent.

"Father Brai! Father Brai!" Drake shouted as he left his tent and entered Father Brai's.

"What? What is it?" he responded, yawning and starting to wake up.

"We need to leave, like now!"

"Why?"

"Darkness is coming!" The moment Father Brai heard those words, he felt Darkness was indeed coming.

"Quickly! We must go!" Father Brai shouted as he grabbed his things. Zack finally woke up with all the commotion going on.

"We need to leave, like now," he told Zack.

"Okay?" Zack thought, confused. Once everyone and everything was out of the camp, the camp started to shift and change back into the black box.

"Quickly, follow me!" Drake said as he took off into the forest.

"Do you know where you are going?" Father Brai asked as him and Zack tried to keep up.

"Yes, Queen Evë showed me in a dream."

"Queen Evë? The Guardian of Light?"

"The very one," he paused, "but we will talk about it later." Shortly, the ruins of the Stone Temple appeared, just like in his dream. Drake started to question whether or not his dream really was a dream or was he really in the Realm of Light? The three hurried into the ruins, not knowing Mr. Anders was right behind them. Drake came to a complete stop next to a remaining wall and looked at the top of it. There, just like in his dream was the Tërcerlin symbol. "Yes! We found it!" Drake said with delight.

"Found what?" Father Brai asked, looking at the wall.

"It's a portal to Jewel City," Drake answered.

"And I want to thank you for finding it for me," Mr. Anders said behind them. The three quickly turned around to find Mr. Anders standing there with his sword drawn towards them. "Now step away from the portal and no one gets hurt."

"Quickly Drake! Take Zack and go! I'll hold him off," Father Brai told Drake, but he didn't move. He suddenly remembered the night in the mountains. This was the man who had killed Father John.

"Drake, let's go!" thought Zack. Drake quickly snapped back, jumped onto Zack's back, and the two darted for the wall. The moment they hit the wall, they went right through it but never came out on the other side. The portal must have worked. Furious, Mr. Anders dashed towards the wall but was stopped by a sword, held by Father Brai and the battle began.

"You think you can take me on, Father Brai?" Mr. Anders said as he chuckled.

"I'm the one who taught you, Mr. Anders," Father Brai responded quickly. Mr. Anders stopped chuckling.

"Then let's finish this!" he shouted as he lunged at Father Brai. *CLINK* Father Brai stopped Mr. Anders' blow. He shoved him off to the left. *CLINK CLINK CLINK* Their swords clashing as Father Brai protected himself first from the left, then the right, then the right again. Then out of nowhere, Father Brai started swinging back; left, right, left, right, right, top, left, left, top, right, right. Mr. Anders kept up and blocked every move Father Brai dished out but he started to get a bit tired. *CLINK CLINK CLINK* Father Brai blocked. *CLINK CLINK CLINK CLINK CLINK* Mr. Anders blocked. Suddenly, Father Brai made a small cut in Mr. Anders' right leg. He dropped instantly. He looked at his wound but only for a moment. As he looked up towards Father Brai and his sword pointed right at him, he noticed the Tërcerlin symbol on the wall start to fade away.

"No!" he shouted as he shot up and towards the wall. The symbol was still barely there when Mr. Anders made it to the wall but it was too late. The portal had closed. He watched as the rest of the symbol disappeared. "You'll pay for this!" he said furiously as he turned around towards Father Brai. Unfortunately, Father Brai was now directly in front of him. He slayed his sword into Mr. Anders' side, not killing him but seriously wounding him.

"I'm sorry, my old friend," he said as he pulled the sword out of Mr. Anders. Father Brai took a few steps back and Mr. Anders fell.

"You'll….you'll….you'll pay….,' he said slowly, covering his wound, trying to stop it from bleeding. Father Brai walked up to him, grabbed his bag, and took a few steps away from him, completely ignoring his warning. Then, he opened his bag and pulled out a large sphere.

"Someone will come for you, I'm sure," Father Brai assured him but all Mr. Anders did was spit in his direction. "Jewel City," he spoke to the sphere and instantly, it started glowing violet. He threw the sphere on the ground in front of him, breaking it open. Just like before, smoke appeared but violet colored this time, surrounding Father Brai. As soon as the smoke cleared, all that remained was Mr. Anders.

Chapter Twelve:

Jessica McGee

When Drake and Zack went through the portal, everything was black for only a moment, then blinding light. After Drake adjusted his eyes, he realized he definitely had arrived in Jewel City. Everything Queen Evë told him was true but he still didn't want to be 'The Chosen One'.

"Let's go," Drake finally said and started walking.

"Where to?" Zack thought.

"We need to find someone named Jessica McGee," Drake answered.

"Okay. Where is she at?"

"Somewhere here in Jewel City. I just don't know where to begin looking…." He stopped speaking as the two turned a street corner. All around them, the buildings were destroyed from the fire, which had all been put out by this point. Dead bodies covered the streets around them, which really started to bother the two. Drake and Zack continued slowly walking, passing by corpse after corpse, neither one saying a word. Before Drake knew it, he was standing in front of what was left of the library. What if the girl he was supposed to find was already dead, he thought to himself.

"Look!" Zack nudged Drake. He looked down the street and saw a girl, around his age, covered in blood, bruises, and torn clothes hiding around the corner of the last building on that street. It was the same girl he saw when Drake and Zack were last in Jewel City.

"Excuse me," Drake shouted towards the girl. She didn't move. "Are you Jessica McGee?" Suddenly, she disappeared around the corner.

"Wait!" he yelled as he took off towards her with Zack following behind. When they got to the corner, part of the building had collapsed due to the fire. They saw the girl enter the building.

"What should we do?" Zack asked. Drake, without answering Zack's question, entered the building. The building was in total disarray and more dead bodies were scattered around. Drake started to wonder what happened to his city and why everyone was dead. Where were his parents and Kim? Were they okay? Were they still somewhere safe? A light flickered from a room ahead. As the two walked into the room, it looked like someone had made that room a home. There was food in one corner and a bed in another. Sitting on the bed was the girl.

"I've been expecting you," the girl said calmly, "Drake Shaw."

"You have?" he asked confusedly.

"Yes, I've been watching you closely for a few years now." Drake thought about it for a moment and slowly remembered seeing her from time to time growing up.

"But why?" he asked.

"When I was only five, there was a terrible accident, which nearly killed me. As I laid dying, a woman in pure white came to me in a dream."

"Queen Evë?" Drake interrupted her, not meaning to.

"Correct. She granted me life, but at a small cost," she pointed at her eyes," I'll be blind for as long as I live. It was the only way to keep me from dying. But throughout the years, my other senses improved dramatically."

"That's really sad to hear," Drake said.

"But there's more. The woman told me that I was to play a huge part in helping a young man who's destined to save the universe from Darkness one day. She told me of the Ancient Five and how crucial it is to find them so I had my parents help me research them."

"We need to find the last two before Darkness does. Do you know how to find them?"

"Well, yes and no."

"Well, it's a start," Drake said as he extended his hand out to her. "Would you be willing to help us out on this journey?" he asked her.

"I would be honored," she said as she shook his hand. Cracking sounds suddenly came from the building.

"Let's get out of here. I think this place is about to collapse," Drake said starting to leave. The other two followed right behind. "This is Zack," he introduced him to Jessica, "he's a shape shifter so don't be alarmed if he changes."

"I won't," she assured him. Just as the three got outside, red smoke started to appear in front of them. Someone was coming, but who? Drake and Zack prepared themselves as Jessica stood behind Drake. As the smoke lifted, there stood Father Brai.

"Now that was some trip," he said, brushing off his robe.

"Father Brai, you're okay!" Drake said with excitement as he ran up to Father Brai and gave him a hug. Father Brai hugged back. Drake was so relieved. After watching his friend Father John die and seeing his new friend Father Brai alive, he felt safe.

"Why wouldn't I be?" he asked with a smile on his face. Drake let go.

"This is Jessica McGee. She will be joining us on this journey," Drake introduced her to Father Brai.

"It's a pleasure meeting you Father Brai," she said.

"As it is meeting you," he replied delightfully.

"I've been studying the locations of the Ancient Five, that were used to trap Lord Taoî's soul," Jessica said. Father Brai looked stunned.

"I'm the protector of the Ancient Five. I've had knowledge of the five passed down from generation to generation until finally it was passed onto me. Shall we discuss things?" he asked her.

"Of course," she replied willingly. "I know where the Stones of Stones are. It's going to be a very tricky and difficult task."

"Ah, the Stones of Stones," Father Brai repeated.

"What are the Stones of Stones?" Drake asked.

"The Stones of Stones are six rounded stones, that when placed together, it's said they will merge into the perfect stone," Jessica said.

"It's said that the stones where scattered all across Evë to prevent them from ever becoming one," Father Brai chimed in. "When you find the first one, it will show you the location of the other five."

"So where do we begin?" Drake asked.

"I've been researching that for years and still no results," Father Brai said shamefully.

"I know where," Jessica said, trying to make Father Brai feel better, "I've read that the first stone is located in a place deep within a forest only known as the Stone Temple." Instantly, Drake remembered his dream. Queen Evë took him there. That's where the portal was. She was showing him a sign.

"I know where that's at!" Drake said, somewhat excited," That place where we just left was the Stone Temple, or what's left of it at least."

"And I just left Mr. Anders there….," Father Brai said in shame.

"That's okay," Drake assured him, "he doesn't know that it's there, does he?"

"No, no he doesn't," Father Brai said, feeling a bit better.

"Then pull out a sphere and let's get going!"

"I can't," Father Brai said, "I'm all out of transporting spheres." Drake let out a deep sigh. He had been traveling on his feet for most of the journey so far and now they had to walk there. All he wanted to do was rest.

"There is another way….," Jessica said, not sounding too happy about it.

"And?" Drake asked. There was a brief moment of silence.

"The Labyrinth of the Archaics," she finally said. Drake had never heard of the Labyrinth of the Archaics but Father Brai sure did. He froze in fear.

"What's the Labyrinth of the Archaics?" Drake asked, trying to break the awkward silence.

"Legends speak on a vast labyrinth built under this entire planet to protect a lost empire who once ruled on the surface, known as the Archaics. When the Great War ended, they hid their empire underground to protect secrets that I don't even know about, but it's said that Darkness found a way into the labyrinth, consuming most of its beauty," Father Brai paused, "I was there once. I was in the Eastern Mountains on a hike one day when I stumbled upon an unusual looking hole in the ground. Somehow, I accidentally fell in, and slid right into the labyrinth. It was dark, cold, and frightening. I heard strange noises and saw several pairs of eyes staring right at me."

"What did you do?" Drake asked, a little scared but very interested.

"I got out of there as fast as I could."

"Is the labyrinth the fastest way there?" Drake asked Jessica.

"I believe so yes," she replied.

"Then I say let's take it. Who knows how much time we have left," Drake said determinedly. Even though the other three didn't want to go that way, they knew he was right.

"Alright then. Quickly, follow me," Jessica finally said. She led them to the library. Once inside, in the center of the library were all the tables and chairs to sit and read books. She pointed out the Tërcerlin symbol engraved into the stone underneath them. "I've never been able to figure out how to open it," she said, kind of confused.

Drake looked at the symbol on his hand. He held it out towards the stone and the two symbols began to glow. Suddenly, the ground started to shake, causing pieces of the destroyed building to fall. The edge of the Tërcerlin symbol on the stone started to rotate. As it rotated clockwise, it rose upward. The tables and chairs were shoved out of the way due to the rising stone. Once it reached about three-fourths of the way up, it stopped. The four noticed a staircase spiraling downward on the inside of the stone. Zack transformed into a phoenix for light.

"I'll go first," Father Brai said as he started down the stairs. Zack and Jessica followed right behind. Drake looked around because he knew something didn't feel right to him. Then, he proceeded down the staircase.

At the bottom, the three were waiting for him. Once Drake got off the last step, the ground started to shake again. The wall with the staircase slowly lowered itself, turning counterclockwise and trapping them in the labyrinth. They looked around. Walls of the labyrinth towered over them; old and dark looking. Pure silence came from the path in front of them. No one had a clue what was down there but they proceeded onward anyway.

Chapter Thirteen:

Labyrinth Of The Archaics

As the four slowly made their way through the labyrinth, no one knew what to expect. "What kind of horrible creatures and beasts live down here," was the only thought that seemed to be running through everyone's minds. They had only gone a few feet into the labyrinth and already Drake wanted to go back. After walking for hours and hitting a few dead ends, they were becoming exhausted.

"Let's take a break," suggested Jessica.

"Good idea," Father Brai agreed. The three stopped but Drake wanted to scout ahead, so he did. Light faded away from behind him as he kept going but light suddenly started to shine from ahead. The closer he got, the brighter it got. Drake quickly ran forward then suddenly stopped dead in his tracks. Ahead of him was an enormous opening. In the center of the opening was a giant temple.

"Hey guys, come quick!" he shouted down the dark corridor. Light shortly appeared as Zack, Jessica, and Father Brai came running to see what was going on. Once the three got to where Drake was, they stopped dead in their tracks, just like Drake did. High above the temple, pockets of light were shining down all over the opening. The temple looked so beautiful; untouched for who knows how many years. The four travelers stood there gazing upon its beauty, except for Jessica who was enjoying the warmth of the light upon her face.

"Is that where we need to go?" Drake finally asked as he pointed towards the temple, "Inside that place?"

"Yes, I think so," Father Brai answered.

"Well, let's get going," Drake said then proceeded forward. Zack transformed into a silver wolf and followed Drake, with Jessica and Father Brai right behind. As they got closer to the temple, they saw a bridge. Below the entire temple looked like an endless pit.

"Watch your step," Father Brai said as they crossed the bridge, "We wouldn't want anyone falling down this hole, would we?" The others laughed a bit. Once across, they walked up to the entrance, but it was blocked by steel bars.

"Now what?" Drake asked. Jessica turned around and started walking back over the bridge. "Wait up!" Drake shouted as he took off towards her. Zack and Father Brai followed shortly behind. The four of them slowly walked around the edge of the pit to the other side.

"This side is blocked too," Zack thought. Zack, Jessica, and Father Brai didn't know what to do. Drake, on the other hand, had an idea. He held out his hand with the Tërcerlin symbol facing upwards, towards the bars. Nothing.

"Well it was worth the shot," Father Brai told Drake. Drake sighed and lowered his hand. Instantly, the bars clanked and started to move. The outer bars went down and the inner bars alternated left and right. Before they knew it, the entrance was opened. They slowly walked into the temple with caution. Though somewhat dark, the building seemed empty. After exploring the temple, the four came to the last room. Nothing.

"There isn't anything here," Drake said with disappointment.

"That's not entirely true child," came a voice from behind them. All four jumped and dashed for the other side of the room. A cloaked figure stood in the doorway.

"Who….who are you?" Drake asked nervously.

"My name is Oshwaia," the figure said.

"What are you?"

"I am an archaic; the last of my people," he said. Relief filled the room, but no one moved. Was this Oshwaia person good or evil was all Drake could ask himself.

"Don't be alarmed. Come," he said as he exited the room. Hesitantly they followed, Drake first, followed by Zack, then Jessica, and finally Father Brai. They followed the figure into a secret room that no one had noticed before. In the center of the room was a large map; a complete layout of the labyrinth.

"I never would have thought I would ever see 'The Chosen One'," Oshwaia said as he walked up to the map and stopped.

"You know me?" Drake asked.

"I know all of you, Drake Shaw," he walked over to Jessica, "Jessica McGee," then to Father Brai, "Father Brai," and finally Zack, "Zack the Seî."

"Then you know why we are here," Drake said as he approached Oshwaia. Oshwaia removed his cloak. He was a tall figure with arms but no legs. He also had no face, but could still hear, smell, see, and speak.

"You seek the Stones of Stones," he started off. "When The Great War ended, Queen Evë showed me the Stones of Stones. But when Darkness threatened this planet a few years ago, I knew hiding the stones here wouldn't be safe anymore."

"So what happened to them?" Jessica asked.

"There are six secret entrances into the labyrinth," Oshwaia started to say.

"And a stone is hidden at each entrance," Father Brai interrupted. Oshwaia didn't reply. "I knew I saw one in the library back in Jewel City. I knew it."

"It is up to you and your friends to retrieve the six stones," Oshwaia said to Drake. The last archaic waved his hand over the map. Six different colored orbs appeared, scattered across the map.

"Each orb is an entrance as well as a stone," Oshwaia pointed out. There was an orange orb that was fairly close to the temple so the four decided to start with that stone.

"What happened to this place?" Father Brai asked Oshwaia as he led them out of the temple.

"Long ago, we hid our great temple underground to protect our secrets. The Labyrinth was made to distract those who sought out our secrets. Soon after, Darkness came from within the heart of Evë, covering most of the labyrinth in it."

He took a breath, "My brothers and I stood outside the temple, prepared for whatever Darkness had in store but….," he paused, "there were too many of them."

"Too many of what?" Jessica asked.

"Demons," he replied. "They were made of blue-essence orbs, protected by a rock-like armor. At first they were easy to defeat, but more came in double the number, then triple. We became vastly outnumbered. I was ordered by our head chief to protect the temple, so I did. I placed a cloaking spell on it, making it undetectable by Darkness and created a powerful protection spell to prevent Darkness from entering," he paused again," I was the only one who survived the attack. My brothers drew the demons deep into the labyrinth, and never returned. I knew from that moment that the stones were no longer safe here, so I snuck each stone to an entrance, hiding them in plain sight for only those who are actually looking for them, will find them."

"What happened to the demons?" Father Brai asked.

"They are still lurking around the labyrinth, so please be careful," Oshwaia warned.

"We will!" Drake assured him. He nodded his head then faded away. They realized they were right back at the entrance of the temple. "Alright, let's go," Drake said, wanting to get this done and over with. As soon as they were all through the entrance, the bars closed behind them. Quietly, the four started off in search of the first stone. After walking for what seemed like hours, they came up to a dead end but with a perfectly rounded opening above.

"Hey, I've been here before," Father Brai said, "this is where I accidentally fell in."

"So how do we get out?" Jessica asked.

"I'm not quite sure. I used a space jumper last time."

"A what?" Drake asked with confusion.

"A space jumper. Space jumpers, or teleporting spheres are those spheres I was using before I ran out."

"Great," Jessica said. They decided to look around for some kind of way out. While searching the walls, Father Brai came across a rock sticking out of the wall. He tried to pull it out, but it didn't budge. He pressed it in and the ground started shaking. From the very beginning of the hole on the surface, a wind vortex started to form, slowly rotating downward towards Drake and his friends. The ground stopped shaking when the vortex was fully formed. Tiny rocks and pebbles slowly lifted and floated to the hole above.

"That must be our way out!" Drake shouted as he pointed towards the vortex. But by activating the way out, they also woke something deep within the Labyrinth.

✧ ✧ ✧ ✧ ✧ ✧ ✧ ✧ ✧ ✧ ✧ ✧

Across the labyrinth, inside a wide opening a monstrous beast slept. When the wind vortex started downward, the creature's blood red eyes opened and then the entire beast suddenly disappeared.

✧ ✧ ✧ ✧ ✧ ✧ ✧ ✧ ✧ ✧ ✧ ✧

As Drake, Zack, Jessica, and Father Brai waited for the vortex to get closer, Drake felt something wrong. He stopped looking up with everyone else and started staring down the corridor. Father Brai noticed Drake's odd expression.

"Drake, what's wrong?" Father Brai asked. His question got Zack and Jessica's attention. The four of them stared into the darkness when the ground started to shake again. Someone or something was coming. Suddenly, the ground stopped shaking and two blood red eyes appeared. Slowly, the eyes pulled forward, revealing the monstrous beast.

"What is that thing?" Zack asked. The beast let out a huge roar. Suddenly, blue essence orbs appeared, and then became covered by a rock-like armor.

"Quillîtars," Father Brai said as he pulled out his sword and prepared for battle. Then blue essence orbs appeared on the walls, and like the ones on the ground, they became covered by a rock-like armor but with wings. "Mînas," Father Brai said, raising his sword.

"Demons?" Drake asked in a very scared tone.

"Yes," Father Brai answered, "and they're being controlled by that Saeî, the monstrous beast behind them all."

"Zack, take Jessica as far back as you can," Drake told Zack.

"Right," he replied as he transformed into a silver wolf and headed over to Jessica. Without questioning or hesitation, she got onto his back and the two got as far back as they could. Then the battle began.

The quillîtars started running towards them. Drake held out his hand and instantly, a ball of fire appeared. Without questioning, he shot the fireball right at the running demons.

"Nice shot!" Father Brai said proudly as some of the quillîtars died from the blast. Just like that, the demons were right in front of the two.

Father Brai swung his sword left and right, up and down as Drake cast fireballs. Meanwhile, the vortex kept approaching downward. Drake and Father Brai were starting to win.

"Look out!" Jessica shouted as she heard a flapping like noise heading right for them and pointed into the sky above them. Drake cast a fireball into the air, where a few mînas were heading right at them. The Saeî stood there, motionless, staring at the battle. More mînas came flying in. Father Brai took care of the quillîtars while Drake dealt with the mînas. Before they knew it, the vortex had reached the ground.

"Run for the vortex!" Drake shouted. Zack and Jessica starting running towards the vortex as Father Brai and Drake did the same, with the quillîtars and mînas after them. Father Brai was the first to jump into the vortex. Instantly, he was sucked up towards the top. "Whatever happens, find those stones," Drake told Zack.

"What are you talking about?" Zack asked. Without answering him, he pushed Zack and Jessica into the vortex. The two were instantly sucked up, just like Father Brai. Drake was about to jump in when something grabbed his arm. He quickly turned to see it was the Saeî who had a hold of him.

"ROOOOAAAAR!" the beast screeched. Drake quickly cast a fireball and shot it at the beast, causing both of them to fly backwards. As Drake quickly got up, the vortex started its ascent upwards. He ran as fast as he could. He jumped for the vortex but barely missed it. As he looked up at the vortex spinning away from him, a hoard of quillîtars and mînas surrounded him, closing inward.

Chapter Fourteen:
Finding The First Stone

The vortex shot Father Brai, Zack, and Jessica out of the hole and onto the mountain side. When the vortex reached the top, the hole collapsed inward, covering itself so no one could enter it from the outside.

"Where's Drake?" Father Brai asked as he got up and brushed off the dust and dirt from his robe. Neither Zack nor Jessica said a word as they got up. The three stood there for a moment, staring at where the hole once was. Father Brai prayed for Drake's safety. "We need to keep moving and find those stones. That's what Drake would want," Father Brai finally said. The other two nodded their heads in agreement. The sun was setting and nightfall would soon be upon them.

Camp was soon set up but no one was happy. They didn't know whether or not Drake was even still alive. Father Brai looked out, over the mountain side. It was quiet and almost peaceful like. Something caught Father Bria's eyes as he was focusing back towards the direction they came from. Something was twinkling in the distance. He got up and headed for it. Zack and Jessica followed. They walked around but the twinkling stopped.

"That's strange," Father Brai said.

"What is?" Jessica asked.

"I swore I saw something twinkling out here," he answered. As the clouds above slowly moved, revealing the moonlight, the twinkling started again. "There!" he shouted as he took off running towards it so he wouldn't lose it again. The other two were right behind. Suddenly, they all stopped. An old stone doorway stood in the middle of an open spot on the mountain side. The twinkling came from a perfectly rounded stone that was at the very top of the doorway.

"Is that….," Zack started to say.

"One of the stones, yes," Father Brai said as he walked up to the doorway. He was too short to reach the stone, so he walked around it, examining the doorway.

Above, more clouds covered the moonlight. Once the moonlight faded away, so did the doorway and the stone.

"What the?" Zack asked with confusion. Father Brai looked up and noticed the clouds covering the moon.

"The doorway is only shown by the moonlight," Father Brai explained as he pointed at the clouds above. More clouds were coming they saw a small opening in the clouds above. They only had one chance to get the stone or they would have to wait a long time for another opportunity.

The moment the moonlight shined through the clouds, the doorway and the stone reappeared. Immediately, Zack lifted Father Brai up and pulled the stone from the doorway, just as the moonlight faded away again. Shortly after, so did the doorway. Father Brai got down and opened his hand, revealing the first stone.

"Yes!" Zack thought with excitement.

"One down, five more to go," Father Brai said as he put the stone away. The three then took off back to their camp to rest and get ready to find the other stones.

Nightfall was approaching as Mr. Anders slowly arrived back at Moonshiar.

"Look who came back empty handed," a soldier laughed as he entered the city. Other soldiers around started to laugh too. Mr. Anders stuck a hand out and all the laughing soldiers went flying backwards into the walls of the buildings. Mr. Anders had always enjoyed using magic, ever since he was a young man, but he couldn't control it sometimes so he hardly used it. The soldiers weren't laughing anymore. He walked through Moonshiar, wounded still from his fight with Father Brai. He headed straight for the temple.

"You have failed me," the shadow said with disappointment.

"I'm sorry your lordship. I almost had him but some kid interfered," Mr. Anders explained as he bowed to his master.

"A kid?" the shadow asked, somewhat intrigued.

"Yes your lordship," Mr. Anders said, still bowing, "a kid with some kind of roundish marking on his hand."

"I no longer have any need for Father Brai. Bring me that child and don't disappoint me again."

"Yes your lordship," he said as he quickly got up and left the room. He hurried back to Moonshiar to prepare and to heal as much of himself as possible. When he got there, he immediately sent his right hand man to Jewel City to capture the child. After healing, Mr. Anders gathered his men and followed behind, just in case things went wrong.

Chapter Fifteen:
The Irrösa Sword

Drake slowly opened his eyes. He looked around and found himself laying on a bed. He got up. Somehow he was back at the temple. He left the room, looking for Oshwaia. He found him laying down.

"Come in child," he said. Drake entered the room and sat next to him.

"What happened?" Drake asked. Oshwaia sat up and turned towards him.

"You were captured," he started off. "The demons took you back to the arena where they have been mostly hiding out. Once they got to the arena, I gave them a surprise they'll never forget. I rescued you and brought you back here."

"Thank you," was all Drake could say.

"There is no need for that. It's an honor to serve 'The Chosen One'." There was a moment of silence. Suddenly, there was a large *Pound* coming from near the entrance of the temple. *Pound* came another. "They are here," Oshwaia said.

"Who's here?" Drake asked.

"The demons. They are trying to get through the protection."

"What do we do?" Drake asked nervously.

"I'm still too weak to fight," Oshwaia paused, "go to the weapons vault in the lower lever of the temple. There, you will need to find the Irrösa Sword. That will protect you."

"Got it!" Drake said with confidence as he left the room. He quickly hurried down the hallway as another *Pound* came. Before he knew it, Drake was standing in front of a giant vault. There was a Tërcerlin symbol at the very top. He stuck out his hand and the Tërcerlin on his hand started to glow.

The vault then unlocked itself and opened. Without any hesitation, Drake hurried into the vault. Once inside, the vault door closed. The vault was so thick he couldn't hear the pounding from outside.

The insanely huge vault was full of piles of gold pieces, gems, and other rare stones. Several swords, bows, and wands were scattered across the vault as well. Drake walked around, trying to figure out which sword was the Irrösa Sword. At the very back of the vault was a statue of Queen Evë holding out a sword.

"That must be it," Drake said out loud. He walked up to the statue and sword. The sword had strange symbols on it. Drake studied it for a moment. He knew it was a phrase but couldn't figure out what language it was in to translate it. Finally, he grabbed the sword. The words started to glow bright green. Suddenly, the vault started to shake. He activated a trap that was set by the

Archaics in case of intruders. The vault stopped shaking and large cracking sounds came from the Queen Evë statue. Drake took a few steps back as the statue slowly rose up. The statue was coming alive. The stone eyes suddenly became blood red and the smile turned into a hatred grin. Two swords flew from out of piles of gold to both of the statue's hands. The statue was definitely alive and wanted Drake dead as it lunged at him, swords swinging.

This was Drake's first battle alone he was beyond scared. The statue swung at Drake. He blocked her first blow but he saw the second sword coming. He pushed the first sword away just in time. He ducked as the second sword swiped above him, barely missing his hair. He got up and ran as fast as he could towards the door. When he got there, nothing he tried would open the door, not even the Tërcerlin on his hand.

Swing came the first sword towards Drake. He dodged out of the way, landing in a gold pile. As he quickly got up, he noticed he uncovered a shield when he landed in the pile. In the center of the shield was a phrase similar to the one on the sword. Out of the corner of his eyes, he saw the statue coming at him with both swords ready to kill.

Clank the swords hit the shield as Drake quickly defended himself. He pushed the swords back and lowered the shield from in front of him. With determination in his eyes, the words on the shield started glowing the same color as the sword. He was ready to defeat this statue or die trying. The statue swung at Drake, but he blocked it with the shield. The second sword came in quick, but again Drake blocked it. Several swings were swung but every single one was blocked.

"Aaaaaaa!" the statue screeched so loud that Drake had to cover his ears. She lunged at him, catching him a bit off guard. He blocked the first sword but the second one cut him on the arm, causing him to drop the shield. Injured, Drake still fought on. Shortly after, he struck a blow that caused the entire arm with the first sword to come off. As soon as it hit the ground, the arm crumbled and the sword just laid there. Drake just found out how to defeat this thing.

"Aaaaaaa!" the statue screeched again. This time, the statue looked very angry. A few more swings were sung towards Drake but he dodged or blocked every one. *Slash* went Drake's sword and so did the second arm, falling and crumbling like the first one. Drake took a running start, jumping into the air and swinging towards the statue's head. As Drake hit the floor, so did the statue's head. Drake quickly got up and turned around towards the stone body. It stood there for a moment then fell right on top of the head, crumbling everything. Drake was finally victorious. He walked up to the shield where he dropped it.

"I could use this too," he said as he picked up the shield. The glowing green light faded away from both items. "The glowing must show when Darkness is near." He put the shield on his back and found a sword pouch. He walked up to the vault door and held out his hand. The Tërcerlin started to glow and the vault door opened. Drake hurried out of the vault, with the door closing and locking behind him. The pounding noise was still ringing through the temple. He ran as fast as he could back to Oshwaia.

"You found it," Oshwaia said with delight, "and the Nitrözi Shield!"

"Yeah," Drake said as he showed the shield to Oshwaia, who immediately noticed the cut on Drake's arm.

"Come here child; let me see your wound." Drake put away the shield and showed him his arm. Oshwaia took his hands and placed them over Drake's wound. A very faint white glow came from between Oshwaia's hands and the wound. Drake flinched a little do to some pain. The glow slowly faded away and Oshwaia removed his hands, revealing no cut. He had healed Drake's wound in order to fight the demons and protect the temple.

"Go," Oshwaia said, "and protect the temple."

"I will!" Drake said determinedly. He ran out of the room and through the temple. The pounding stopped just before Drake got to the entrance. As he exited the temple, the demons had broken through the protection. There was a small hole where a few quillîtars were coming through. The bars closed behind him. Drake took a deep breath, got a good grip on both the sword and the shield, and dove into battle.

Clash Clink Drake sliced one quillîtar after another, making his way through the protection spell and drawing the demons away from the temple. Inside, Oshwaia tried to fix the protection on the temple. Once Drake broke through the rock-like armor, he could strike their essence orbs, releasing the essence inside into the air and instantly killing them. Drake was starting to get an advantage when the mînas came in. Silently, they flew in from the shadows but Drake was ready for them. He stuck his hand out and shot fireballs at them, completely catching them by surprise. Once the fireballs hit the rock-like armor, it instantly evaporated, dropping their essence orbs. Just like the quillîtars, he could slice open the orbs, killing them. Drake was definitely winning this battle until *Swish* came a sword from the darkness ahead, surprising Drake who barely escaped the blow. The Saeî came out of the shadow and wanted in on this fight.

"ROOOOAAAAR!" the beast screeched.

"Not you," Drake said. With four-arms, a lizard-like body, and lion-head the beast looked like all it wanted to do was to destroy everything in its path. The Saeî pulled its arm back, revealing not just one sword, but four; one in each hand.

"ROOOOAAAAR!" the beast screeched again.

"You've got to be kidding me!" Drake said in agitated disappointment, then he lunged at the monstrous beast. Immediately, Drake won the "first round" by cutting off one of its arms.

"Aaaaaaa!" the beast screeched in pain. More quillîtars and mînas attacked. Drake wished his friends were there to help. Somehow, Drake managed to keep killing more demons while protecting himself from the Saeî. *Slash* Drake struck a blow across the beast's chest, revealing a blue-essence orb, just like the other demons only much larger.

"Aaaaaaaaaaaaa!" the Saeî screeched, echoing across the entire labyrinth. Drake had made the beast very angry now. More quillîtars and mînas appeared. By this point, Drake started to become tired and weak.

"Someone, please help me!" he thought to himself.

"Use the power of the Irrösa Sword and the Nitrözi Shield," came Oshwaia's voice from inside Drake's head.

"But….," he paused, "but how?"

"Use the Light that is inside you."

"Use the Light that is inside of me?" Drake
said out loud. Suddenly, the phrases on both the
sword and shield began glowing bright green, like
before. "Use the Light that is inside of me!"
shouted Drake. The glow on the sword and shield
grew brighter and brighter as did Drake's strength.
He charged right for the Saeî, killing any demon
that got in his way. The Saeî swung the first blow
but Drake ducked and immediately cut off that
arm. *Swish Swish* the Saeî swung twice. The first
one Drake dodged and the second one, Drake used
the shield, instantly stopping the blow. He pushed
it away, jumping into the air, and cutting off the
two remaining arms. The beast fell to its knees in
pain. Drake killed a few more quillîtars and mînas
that headed his way. Then *Slash* he sliced the Saeî
across the chest again, barely hitting the orb.

"Crap!" Drake said to himself with
disappointment. He didn't even make a scratch on

it. Suddenly, the orb changed from blue to green and everything stopped, as if time suddenly froze. The quillîtars and mînas suddenly vanished without a trace. Then the Saeî slowly started to turn to dust starting from the bottom upward, leaving only the now green-essence orb, which fell onto the pile of dust that once was the monstrous beast. Drake took his sword, stood over the orb, and was about to strike a blow.

"No, it's not worth it," he said as he lowered his sword and stepped away, placing the sword into its holder. The orb suddenly shrunk to carrying size. Drake walked up to it and picked it up.

"You have spared me," came the Saeî's voice from inside the orb. Drake just stared at it. "I am now forever in your debt, master."

"Master?" Drake said, "What are you talking about? I don't serve the Darkness, I only serve the Light." There was no response. The glow on the sword and shield faded away. After catching his breath and gathering some energy, he hurried back to Oshwaia.

Chapter Sixteen:

Reuniting Friends

"Oshwaia!" shouted Drake as he entered the room. Oshwaia wasn't there.

"My child," Oshwaia said from behind Drake, who immediately turned around. "I'm so relieved to see you alive."

"It's great to see you are doing well too," Drake responded, "oh, here." He pulled out the green-essence orb and handed it to Oshwaia.

"He is your demon now," Oshwaia said as he refused the orb.

"What do you mean he's mine?" Drake asked, confused.

"Come," Oshwaia said as he left the room. Drake followed. Shortly after, they were in the temple's library. Oshwaia ran along several book shelves until he finally stopped at one.

"Ahh, here we are," he said as he pulled a book out by its top corner, revealing it as a lever. At the very end of the library, a bookshelf pushed forward and moved to the side, revealing a spiraling staircase leading downward. Oshwaia started down first. As soon as both of them were on the staircase, the bookshelf moved back into place. Drake was simply amazed how not a single book fell. The only light they had was the green-essence orb, glowing just the right amount of light to see. Oshwaia started down the stairs.

"Why do we have to be closed in here?" Drake asked as he followed.

"I was unable to restore the protection spell," Oshwaia paused.

"Yeah, but they fled. They're gone."

"You are correct, but only to gain their numbers. They will be back in even greater numbers. The sole purpose of those fowl demons is to retrieve the Stones of Stones. Once they come back, they will completely destroy the protection spell, and search the temple from top to bottom to find the stones, destroying anything that stands in their way."

"But the stones aren't here."

"You are correct again, but they don't know that."

"So why don't you just put up another protection spell?"

"Neither one of us nor the two of us together are strong enough to protect the temple."

"So is this an escape route?" Drake asked with a little excitement in his voice.

"No child, but it will give us some time. Come." Oshwaia answered as he exited the staircase into a corridor.

"Oh," Drake said with disappointment then followed Oshwaia. It was a dead end, but Oshwaia kept on going right through the wall. Drake slowly walked up to it. Can I go through it too or was this another one of Oshwaia's disappearing acts? Drake thought to himself. He took a deep sigh then slowly pushed his hand against the wall. His hand slowly fell through the wall so Drake took a step forward and walked through the wall. Inside was a hidden room, small and dark. Drake took a few steps forward when suddenly, the ground started to glow. He looked down to see the Tërcerlin symbol engraved into the ground

"Ahh good, it works," Oshwaia said joyfully.

"What works?" Drake asked, a bit nervous.

"The Tërcerlin Teleporter."

"The Tёrcerlin Teleporter?"

"Yes. This teleporter will take you anywhere you would like to go on Evё."

"What about you?"

"I will be fine," Oshwaia assured him.

"No!" Drake said firmly. "Those things will be back and will show no mercy. I'm not losing another friend."

"You....you consider me a friend?" Oshwaia asked curiously.

"Of course I do!" Drake said proudly with a smile on his face. He extended a hand out towards Oshwaia.

"I haven't left in so long," Oshwaia said nervously. Drake didn't budge. Slowly, Oshwaia grabbed Drake's hand and got on the teleporter. "Where to?" he asked.

"To where my friends are," Drake said determinedly. Suddenly, the outer glow of the

Tërcerlin symbol showed a beam of light as high as the ceiling and became so bright that Drake had to cover his eyes.

Jessica, Zack, and Father Brai slowly walked back into the now dead town of Jewel City.

"I wonder what happened here," Father Brai said.

"Something doesn't feel right," Zack thought.

"I agree with Zack. Something definitely doesn't feel right here," Jessica chimed in.

"Now that you two say something about it," agreed Father Brai until Zack heard something and stopped dead in his tracks, causing Father Brai to lose his concentration.

"What's up?" Father Brai asked.

"I…I hear…I hear…someone….," Zack thought, listening, "someone….someone looking for help!" Zack shot off towards the yelling person.

"I hear it too!" Jessica said, as her and Father Brai tried to keep up with Zack as he dashed through the city.

"Aaaaaaa!" screamed a female's voice up ahead, causing Father Brai and Jessica to run even faster. When they finally caught up with Zack, he had a girl about Drake's and Jessica's age trapped in a corner.

"It's okay. I'm not going to hurt you," Zack thought to the girl. She just screamed again.

"You're terrifying her," Jessica said as she approached Zack.

"I'm sorry," she said to the girl, "my friend here can be a bit obnoxious"

"Ththththat thing is your friend?" the girl asked nervously.

"I'm your friend?" Zack thought.

"Yes, he's my friend," Jessica answered, ignoring Zack. "What's your name?" she asked the girl.

"Kim....my name is Kim," she answered.

"Are you alone Kim?" Father Brai asked as he joined Jessica and Zack.

"Yeah," she said, not really wanting to admit it.

"Tell us what happened," Father Brai said, trying to gain Kim's trust.

"Well....," she started, "it all started when my ignorant yet caring friend Drake and I left the city for a while."

"Drake?" Zack thought curiously.

"Drake who?" Father Brai asked.

"Drake Shaw. Why? Do you know him? Where is he? Is he okay?" Kim asked frantically.

"It's okay, it's okay," Jessica said as she approached Kim. "Everything will be alright." Father Brai and Zack joined the girls. "Drake is fine. In fact, we will be meeting up with him soon if you'd like to join us," she said, hoping inside she was right.

"Um….," Kim said, trying not to stare at Jessica's eyes. She noticed she was blind. "Sure."

"Great, then that's settled. Let's get back to finding those stones," Father Brai said eagerly as he took off.

"What stones?" Kim asked.

"We'll explain on the way," Jessica assured her but deep down she wondered what truly happened to Drake. Was he hurt? Was he alive? Father Brai and Zack were thinking the same thoughts. The three followed right behind Father Brai.

"So where are we going?" Kim asked.

"To the library," Father Brai said.

"For what? A book?" Kim asked, confused.

"No silly, the stone."

"What stone?" Now, she was really confused.

"I don't want to overwhelm you right now but we are looking for six stones that have been scattered all over Evë," Jessica explained.

"Why?"

"You know the stories of Light and Darkness, don't you?"

"Yeah."

"Well, all of it is true and those stones are part of a key, and if Darkness gets ahold of them, it could mean the end of life itself," Farther Brai butted in.

"Oh….," was all Kim could say.

"Don't take it personally. It's just something we have to do," Jessica said to Kim, trying to reassure her.

"I know. I just wasn't expecting that overwhelming of an explanation," replied Kim.

"That's Father Brai for you. Oh, and that's Zack," she said as she pointed at Zack.

"It has a name?" Kim whispered to Jessica, who started to laugh quietly.

"Yes, IT has a name. He won't hurt you though," she whispered back, "I promise."

"Okay," whispered Kim.

"And I'm Jessica," Jessica said normally.

"Father Brai, Zack, and Jessica, got it," she said as the four arrived at the library. They slowly entered.

"So what exactly does this stone look like?" Kim asked.

"It's a perfectly rounded stone, like this one," Father Brai said as he showed her the first stone. "I can't exactly remember where I saw it but if we look hard enough, we'll find it!" he said with confidence as he started to look for the second stone. The other three joined in shortly afterwards. They searched and searched but had no luck.

"Maybe someone has found it already," Kim finally said as she gave up and stopped looking.

"Kim may have a point," Jessica agreed and stopped looking.

"So then what do we do?" Father Brai asked as he too stopped looking. As the three tried to figure out what to do next, Zack kept looking.

All the way at the very back of the library, up towards the ceiling was a stone statue of Queen Evë (almost identical to the one Drake fought in the labyrinth's vault). On her head was a crown and in the center was a perfectly rounded and smooth stone.

"Father Brai! Jessica! Kim! Come quick!" Zack thought as loud as he could. The three ran as fast as they could to the back of the library.

"What is it Zack?" Jessica asked as they arrived.

"There!" he pointed at the stone with his nose.

"The second stone," Father Brai said with delight.

"So how do we get the stone down from there?" Kim asked.

"Allow me," Zack thought as he transformed into a phoenix and headed for the stone. Kim screamed with fear when Zack transformed.

"It's okay," Jessica quickly comforted her. "It's okay. That's normal for him. See, he really isn't a silver wolf. He's really a Seî," she said a bit cautiously. Jessica had always been a bit suspicious about Zack. Something about him was off to her.

"What's a Seî?" Kim asked.

"It's a creature that can transform into other creatures," Father Brai explained. Zack reached out with its mouth and touched the stone. The moment he touched it, a beam of light appeared from the statue's eyes. The light aimed right at the Tërcerlin symbol in the center of the library, where they entered the labyrinth. Then the entire symbol started to glow and the eyes stopped. The glow on the outer ring became a beam of light so high it nearly hit the ceiling and become so bright that everyone had to close their eyes. Then it stopped, just like that. Zack grabbed the stone and quickly joined the others, handing off the stone to Father Brai. The four hurried over to the center to find Drake and Oshwaia standing in the center of the symbol.

"Drake!" Kim shouted as she ran towards him.

"Kim?" Drake asked, confused. "What, what are you doing here?" She ran up to him and hugged him tightly.

"We found her outside looking for help," Jessica said as she approached them. Kim noticed Oshwaia, screamed, turned Drake around, and held him in front of her, like a shield.

"What the heck is that thing?" she screamed. Drake immediately turned around and grabbed her.

"It's okay, it's okay. He's not going to hurt you, I promise," he said calmly.

"You, you sure?" she said a bit nervously.

"Yes, I'm sure," he assured her. He moved to the side of her. "Kim, this is Oshwaia. Oshwaia, this is my best friend Kim," he introduced them.

"It is a pleasure to meet you," Oshwaia said.

"Likewise," Kim said, still a bit nervous.

"It's so good to have you back Drake," Jessica said.

"Thank you. It's good to be back. I missed you all," Drake replied. He paused a moment. "So Kim? Why are you here? Father John told me you and my parents fled to Crystral," Drake started.

"Sorry to interrupt but can she tell you on the way?" Father Brai interrupted, "we only have two stones and I'm sure Darkness is out there looking for the other ones."

"He does have a point Drake," thought Zack.

"You're right," Drake said, "Kim? I'm sorry but explain to me on the way, okay?"

"Okay," she said. As the six of them left the library, Drake began to worry inside. Not only was Father Brai, Zack, and Jessica in danger of getting hurt (or worse), but now so was Kim and Oshwaia.

"So you have the stones from Jewel City and the Eastern Mountains, correct?" Oshwaia said as they finally reached outside the library.

"Yes, that is correct," Father Brai said as he held them out. Oshwaia magically pulled out a box from within his robe. He opened it. Inside, there were six spots where each stone could be placed. Father Brai placed the two stones inside the box. Oshwaia closed the box and put it away.

"Now, we must head back to the Eastern Mountains," Oshwaia said.

"What? Why?" Father Brai asked confusedly.

"I'll explain on the way, after Kim tells us her story," he said as he began the journey. The other five followed and the six were off not knowing but for the third stone.

Chapter Seventeen:

Finding More Stones

"Father John stopped me on my way to your parent's house," Jessica began. "He told me something bad was going to happen in Jewel City very soon and that I needed to hurry and meet up with your parents. He told me he knew where you were and that you were safe," she said directly towards Drake. "Then he told me that the three of us were to leave town immediately, and follow the roads towards Crystral. There, we would be safe. At first, I didn't want to believe this guy but when I got to your place, your parents were packing a few things and said that the three of us needed to leave. That's when I knew Father John was telling me the truth. We were just about to leave when we heard what sounded like bombs going off. We ran outside and smoke appeared in the sky ahead of us. More bombs went off and more smoke appeared, but closer to us this time. I took your parents to that hole you found in the wall. We quickly went through it and into the forest as more bombs went off. I could see flames rising up the buildings as we entered the forest. We hurried along the road until we got to a fork and headed towards Deller's Pass, which led towards Crystral." She paused to catch her breath.

"By the time we reached the fork, it was almost nighttime and we didn't have anywhere to sleep. So we all cuddled next to a fire your father made. At the first sign of light, we were on the move again, hurrying as fast as we could. Once we got to Deller's Pass, we could see Crystral. We thought we would be safe, like Father John said but then things took a turn for the worse."

"What happened?" Drake interrupted her, really wanting to know.

"When we got there, it was mid-afternoon. It seemed very quiet and peaceful when this one lady appeared out of nowhere. She pulled out a sword and started to threaten us. Your father," she paused again, "your father managed to distract her while your mother and I tried to get away, but somehow she captured your mother and father. I managed to slip by her and got away. I'm so sorry Drake." Kim's eyes started to fill with tears.

"It's okay," Drake told her, comforting her.

"I don't know who she was, but she looked very bad and dangerous." Drake thought to himself that this kidnapper must have been working for Darkness and knew he was 'The Chosen One'. There was a bit of silence as no one knew what to say next. Finally, Father Brai broke the awkwardness.

"So why are we heading back to the Eastern Mountains?" he asked, trying to make it seem casual.

"Long ago, before Darkness came, before Queen Evë, before any of this….we were a thriving race, living above ground. Using the peace within the universe to survive. Everything was good until," Oshwaia started off.

"Until King Orzoîrk fired the Murcurî Cannon and destroyed Zoigë," Drake interrupted.

"That's correct," Oshwaia continued. "When Zoigë was destroyed, it released a terrible curse upon this planet, nearly wiping out our species. Only a few dozen and myself survived. Together, we took our mighty temple and forced it underground, hoping to hide it from Darkness forever," Oshwaia paused a moment. The sun was going down and soon it would be night. "Let's find the shoreline and set up camp for the night."

"But can't you finish your story first?" Kim asked, almost begging.

"Later child," he said, "come." Shortly afterwards, the six found the shoreline and with the magic from both Father Brai and Oshwaia, a fully protected campsite was ready.

After eating and relaxing, everyone gathered around the fire and Oshwaia's story continued.

"So what happened with you, your brothers, and the temple?" Kim asked eagerly. At first, he did not respond. He just sat there, in silence.

"….There was a cost to protecting our temple," he finally started off. "Most of my brothers sacrificed their magic to put the temple underground. After all my brothers died trying to protect the stones, I used most of what magic I had left to hide the stones."

"But where do we come in?" Father Brai asked, "How did we get put here?"

"Oh yes, I completely forgot. When the temple was fully underground, my brother Rimerkei used the rest of his magic to cover up the ground where the temple once proudly stood."

"Why did you force the temple underground to begin with?" Drake asked.

"When Queen Evë first came to us, she told us in order to destroy the curse for good, the land above ground would have to be completely destroyed and a new species would take our place," Oshwaia answered, "your species….but when everything above ground got destroyed, somehow four portals remained."

"Portals?" Father Brai asked, confused.

"Yes, they were archways that were scattered across the planet that could teleport you from one archway to another. I hid a stone at each archway and I might just be able to activate the portals again."

"Thank goodness! My feet are killing me," Kim complained. Everyone but her started laughing. "What? I'm serious!" she continued to complain. After saying their good nights, everyone headed off to bed except Drake. He only pretended to fall asleep until everyone else was. Once they were asleep, he crept out of his tent and took off on a walk. He started down the shoreline, staring at the almost full moon. Beyond the moon was Darkness. Drake tried to imagine what it was like before Darkness; the other planets, moons, suns, and even stars.

"One day," he said, "I wish to be able to see the universe the way it was." He suddenly noticed he had walked too far away from the campsite and turned around. He noticed an island off in the distance. He wanted a quick look at the island so he ran up the shore towards the base of the mountains. When he got there, he saw something he wasn't expecting; an object just up the mountain side. He followed up the side and suddenly stumbled upon an archway. Drake stood there for a moment, checking out its symbols and marks.

"Way to go Drake. You found it!" came a voice from behind him. He immediately turned around, attempting to draw his sword but it wasn't on his back. Jessica was holding his sword.

"Don't scare me like that, geese!" Drake said with annoyance, but still glad it was Jessica.

"Don't take off like that," she said, handing back his sword.

"Deal," he agreed as he took his sword and put it away.

"One of us needs to go get the others while the other one stays here and watches."

"Good idea," Drake agreed.

"I'll stay," Jessica said.

"Are you sure cause I can stay and," he started to say.

"Yes, now hurry," she interrupted.

"Okay," Drake said and headed back to the shoreline. He ran down the shore back to the campsite. "Father Brai! Oshwaia! Kim! Zack! Come quick!" he shouted as he neared the campsite, "Hurry hurry hurry!"

"What is it?" Father Brai asked as he slowly came out of his tent. Oshwaia, Kim, and Zack shortly joined him. Drake ran up to the four and caught his breath.

"We found a portal," he finally said.

"We?" Kim asked.

"Yeah, Jessica and I. She's there right now so we have to hurry."

"Okay, let's go!" Father Brai said. The five hurried down the shoreline, with Drake leading. Drake soon recognized the spot where he first noticed the island.

"There!" he shouted, pointing towards the base of the mountains. They all shifted and headed upwards. Shortly, they spotted Jessica standing in front of the archway.

"Good job you two," Father Brai said as they approached Jessica.

"Actually, Drake found it. I was just following him," Jessica responded.

"Following him?" Father Brai asked, confused and concerned. Meanwhile, while the three communicated with each other, Oshwaia walked up to the archway. There was a large opening, surrounded by cylinder pillars. Below was three buttons and inside the opening was the third stone. Oshwaia pushed all three buttons at once and the cylinder pillars disappears downwards. Then he turned towards the others.

"I couldn't sleep so I went for a walk," Drake continued.

"You know it's not safe to be alone Drake," Father Brai scolded Drake.

"Drake is much stronger than you give him credit for," Oshwaia interrupted as he walked up to everyone. "Child, may I see your demon orb?"

"Of course," Drake said as he pulled out the green-essence orb and handed it to Oshwaia.

"What is that?" Kim asked.

"Yeah, what is that?" Zack asked too.

"It's a demon's essence," Drake answered, "it's a long story." Oshwaia took the orb. He first removed the firth stone and replaced it with Drake's demon orb. Finally, he pressed the three buttons together again, enclosing the orb.

Instantly, it began to float when a green misty spiral appeared inside the archway.

"Now that is better," Oshwaia said as he put the third stone away.

"You activated the portal," Drake replied.

"Actually, I activated all four of them."

"Way to go!" shouted Kim with excitement.

"Well let's get going," Father Bria suggested.

"Let's rest and we can travel in the morning." Drake said.

"But how will be find the archway again in the morning?" Jessica asked.

"When I activated it, the protection spells I placed on them ended, allowing us to find them at any time," Oshwaia replied.

"I agree with Drake then," Kim said.

"Same here," Jessica agreed too. Oshwaia opened the compartment, took the orb out, closed it, and handed the orb back to Drake. The moment the compartment opened, the spiral and glowing faded away.

"Protect it," Oshwaia said as he handed back the orb, "that power source is strong enough to not only power one archway, but all four of them at the same time"

"I will," Drake assured him. The six headed back to rest and prepare for travel in the morning.

As the morning came and the sun began to rise, Drake woke up with excitement but he had an off feeling. After everyone was up and fed, the campsite was put away and they headed for the portal.

"I will go first," Oshwaia said as he took the orb from Drake and activated the portal.

"How do we shut down the portal once we are all through it?" Drake asked.

"We don't," Oshwaia replied, "the only way to close the portal is to remove the power source from the archway we use it in."

"How do we activate the other portals though? Do we need more orbs?" Kim asked.

"No child. The orb Drake possesses has enough power to activate all four portals at one time," Oshwaia spoke as he approached the portal.

"Will I get the orb back?" Drake asked.

"Yes child, once we achieve our goal," he paused, "one thing you all need to know before you go through is only one person at a time can enter the archway and into the portal. Any more than that may result in serious consequences."

"Understood," Father Brai assured him. The others agreed as well. Oshwaia stepped into the archway and instantly, the portal sucked him into the spinning vortex. Then, he was gone.

"Alright," Father Brai started, "who's next?" Drake started to notice how Father Brai liked to take charge and laughed a little inside because he knew he would eventually be the true leader.

"I guess I'll go," Kim said. She took a deep breath and headed into the archway and into the portal and just like Oshwaia, she was gone. Zack went next, followed by Father Brai.

"Ladies first," Drake offered.

"I know what you're planning on doing," she refused.

"What do you mean?" he asked, confused.

"Once I went through, you were going to take out the power source. I can read deep thoughts, remember."

"I was," he said, telling her the truth.

"I don't think so!" Jessica demanded.

"But….," Drake started off.

"I said no!" she said almost angrily. "I will go through first, but you better be right behind me!"

"Okay, okay," Drake said finally. Jessica was just about to enter the archway when she suddenly stopped due to Drake's screaming.

"Get off me!" he shouted as a strange man grabbed him from behind. Jessica shoved the man off of Drake. The two prepared themselves for a fight as the man stood up and started laughing.

"Who are you?" Drake demanded to know.

"Captain Ric's the name and my boss wants you boy," the man said.

"And who's your boss?" Jessica asked.

"Why, Christopher Anders of course." That name sounded familiar to Drake. He thought to himself where had he heard that name then suddenly, he remembered. He remembered first hearing about him from Father John, then again when he killed Father John. The man never even saw his own death coming. Drake started to cry a little.

"Remember him?" Captain Ric said towards Drake, "he's the one who murdered your friend; oh what was his name? Father John perhaps?" Drake instantly got angry at Captain Ric and was about to lunge at him when Jessica stopped him.

"I'll keep him busy while you go get help," Drake demanded.

"Okay," she said without any hesitation but just as she turned to run towards the portal, Captain Ric appeared behind the two. He shoved Drake backwards, causing him to stumble and fall. But as he fell, he fell into the archway. Instantly, the portal took a hold of Drake and started pulling him in. "Jessica!" he shouted as he entered the portal and vanished.

Drake's eyes finally adjusted and he found himself back at the Stone Temple where he first met Queen Evë. He immediately turned around only to see the portal closing.

"Jessica!" he shouted as he darted towards the portal, but it was too late. He entered the archway full right through it.

"What's going on Drake? Where's Jessica?" Father Brai asked as he helped Drake get back up.

"We were attacked," Drake said as he stared at the archway.

"By who?" Zack asked.

"Captain Ric," Drake said slowly as he continued to stare at the archway.

"Captain Ric?" Father Brai repeated.

"One of Mr. Anders' henchmen," Drake replied.

"Who is Mr. Anders?" Kim asked, somewhat confused.

"He's the right hand man to Michael Cashner, and the same man who was shooting at Zack and I back when Father John, well, you know."

"What happened to Father John?" Kim asked.

"He was murdered," Drake replied.

"Oh," was all she could say.

"Michael Cashner is also number one on the most wanted," Father Brai remembered. Thanks to him, Kim also remembered something about Michael Cashner.

"It was him," Kim said in a serious tone.

"What do you mean?" Drake asked, confused. He turned around and looked at her.

"When I was trying to get away, I got cut off. I was running through the forest when I first heard your mother calling for me, as though she got away. I stopped and listened. Then your father started calling for me too. The next thing I knew I was looking for them, calling to them and trying to find them. I found the path that lead away from Deller's Pass. It sounded like they escaped and were on the path somewhere. I ran further away from the pass, but I didn't know I was running into a trap." she paused to catch her breathe. Everyone was now focusing on her story.

"Up ahead, I saw your parents standing there, but with a man standing right behind them. I immediately stopped. Your parents then shouted for me to run back into the forest as fast as I could. I took off as fast I could, but I was being chased; actually more like hunted. That girl who first captured your family was after me. I ran as fast as I could with her hot on my trail until I got to the river. I swam across as fast as I could but that girl stopped at the river; she never chased me across.

I'm so sorry Drake. I'm sorry I didn't remember this until now."

"It's okay," Drake said.

"But the man who truly has your parents is," Kim started to say.

"Michael Cashner. Michael Cashner has my parents," Drake interrupted.

"I'm so sorry Drake!" Kim begged for forgiveness as she hugged him.

"It's okay," he said as he hugged her back, "it's not your fault." He turned and looked at the archway, hoping Jessica was alright.

Chapter Eighteen:

Change In Fate

The five stood there, watching for a sign, a glimmer of hope, something. But there was nothing. After Oshwaia got the stone from the archway, everyone but Drake started to leave. Drake just knew Jessica was okay and he was about to be proven right. He finally turned and barely started to walk away when suddenly, the portal started up. Someone was about to come through but who? The others quickly joined Drake as he turned around and took a few steps back. Father Brai and Drake stood in front of Zack, Kim, and Oshwaia, with swords drawn as they readied themselves for whatever was coming. Then, a body appeared inside the portal and Jessica came walking out of the archway, tired and exhausted.

Drake immediately ran up to her just as she started to collapse.

"Thank goodness you are okay," Oshwaia said as the others quickly joined the two.

"Yeah, I'm fine," Jessica said as she stood back up, "thanks Drake."

"No problem," he replied, "but what happened to Captain Ric?"

"Well, after you went through the portal, I quickly pushed the three buttons, which closed the portal. Captain Ric got very angry and tried to come after me, but I was too fast for him. I kept dodging him until he trapped me. I got scared and held my hands out when all of a sudden, something strange happened to me. I felt something warm in my palms then without warning, the warm feeling intensified dramatically then it just disappeared, as did Captain Ric."

"You mean he just vanished?" Kim asked.

"I guess," Jessica said. They were all relieved that Captain Ric was gone but they weren't out of the woods yet. Darkness now knew what they were up to and Drake knew that if they didn't pick up their pace, Darkness would get the remaining stones and the last artifact. Drake explained his idea about splitting up into groups to find the remaining stones. Once it was all settled, Drake and Zack went back through the portal but shortly realized that they weren't at the same archway as before.

"What the?" Zack started off.

"The portals must be designed to teleport to different portals," Drake interrupted. "Do you trust me?"

"Of course," Zack replied.

"Then stay here," Drake said as he ran right into the portal. Moments later, he found himself in the same forest as just a while ago, but at a different archway. He heard a faint noise in the distance. He listened closely. It was the others; they must have been nearby. He turned back towards the archway and looked for the stone. Along the side of the archway, something shiny caught Drake's eyes. He ran up to it.

"Another stone," he said out loud. He quickly grabbed it then headed towards his friends.

"So what do we do now?" Kim asked.

"Well, we need to come up with a plan first," answered Father Brai.

"I agree with Father Brai," Oshwaia agreed.

"Okay," Kim said. Suddenly, she heard a small ruffling noise. "What was that?" she asked, a bit nervous.

"I didn't hear anything," Father Brai said.

"I did," Jessica replied.

"Boo!" Drake shouted as he popped out behind Kim.

"Aaaaaaa!" she screamed as she ran and hid behind Father Brai. Instantly, Drake busted out laughing. Once they realized it was Drake everyone else but Kim started to laugh as well. "That wasn't funny Drake," she said, pissed off.

"I thought it was," he replied as he stopped laughing.

"How did you get here? I thought you went through the portal with Zack?" Father Brai asked.

"It doesn't matter," Drake said as he handed Oshwaia the stone he found. "Now, here's the plan," he started off. "All of you go through the portal. Zack is waiting on the other side. Once you all get there, wait for me. Okay? Trust me." Then, he took off running into the trees, disappearing.

"I trust him," Jessica said as she ran through the portal.

"As do I," Oshwaia said then followed after Jessica.

"After you," instated Father Brai to Kim.

"Thank you," she said and entered the portal, followed by Father Brai.

Drake stood there, staring at the Ku Islands. It seemed so peaceful there, yet Drake could see deep within the island, a dark, thick fog hovered over something dark. Drake wanted to go see what it was, but realized his friends were waiting for him so he just ignored it, for now. He shook himself and concentrated. He started looking for the archway and soon found it. As he walked up to the archway, he noticed something weird near it. He found a pile of ash, as though someone had recently poured it there. Drake couldn't figure it out. He knelt down next to it and touched it. Suddenly, a strange feeling came over Drake. *Captain Ric* rang in his head. He immediately let go of the ashes, got up, and took a few steps back. The name stopped ringing and the feeling disappeared. Something really strange was going on and Drake didn't like it one bit. He turned around, forgetting about the ashes and headed into the portal to join his friends yet again.

As the others came through the portal, Zack was extremely happy.

"Where's Drake?" Zack asked.

"He'll be here, trust me," Jessica assured him. Everyone but Drake was now finally through the portal.

"Good," came a voice behind the archway, "now I can finally destroy all of YOU at one time." Out walked Mr. Anders. Suddenly, his men popped out from behind the surrounding rocks and trees with swords drawn towards the five. They were surrounded. Father Brai drew his sword when Mr. Anders started to chuckle. "You really think you can defeat me?" he asked.

"When Drake gets here," Kim started to say as she hid behind Zack.

"When Drake gets here," Mr. Anders interrupted, "none of you will be!" Suddenly, the men threw small black balls at Zack and the others, instantly exploding. They released a black smoke, causing them to start coughing.

"You'll never....*cough*....get away....*cough cough*....with this," Father Brai said as he coughed.

"Oh, but I will," replied Mr. Anders. One by one, each of the five fell to the ground, unconscious.

"Sleeping....," Father Brai started to say but couldn't finish as he fell to the ground asleep.

"Smoke," Mr. Anders finished, "get them out of here," he said with disgust. Some of the men, who were wearing masks, rushed in and grabbed the sleeping bodies. Mr. Anders walked up to the closest rock to the portal and attached a scroll to it and began to chuckle again. "Foolish child," he said as his chuckle turned into an evil laugh.

As Drake finally came through the portal, he looked around, but no one was there.

"Hello?" he called out, "anyone there?" There was no response. "Zack?" he paused, "Jessica? ANYONE" There was still no response. It seemed like everyone just disappeared. Drake started to look for the others. "Kim?" he shouted as he looked, "Father Brai?" No one was answering him. "Oshwa….," he started to say when he

241

noticed something. On the closest rock to the archway hung a scroll. He detached the scroll and began reading it....

You have put up a pretty good fight so far. I'm quite impressed. You have such great potential yet you waste it on the Light. Have the remaining stones and the last artifact in three days when the sun sits high noon. Meet me where we first met with the items or you'll never see your friends again. Your choice.

C.A.

Drake immediately dropped the scroll. The man who killed Father John now had the rest of his friends. For the first time in a while, Drake felt truly terrified. He had no idea what to do or where to go for help. He was now all alone.

Not knowing what exactly to do, Drake made himself a fire and collected food. As evening came, Drake sat in front of his fire.

"What do I do?" he asked himself. As the evening turned to night and the fire slowly smoked away, Drake slowly fell asleep.

Drake's eyes opened, wide awake. It seemed like it was daytime but brighter. He was back in the Realm of Light. He got up and looked around. Everything seemed normal. He took off towards the archway and there was Queen Evë again.

"I'm so sorry Queen Evë," Drake said as he ran up to her.

"Don't be Drake," she said, "It is not your fault. Fate has a bigger role for you yet."

"What do you mean?" he asked, confused and shocked.

"See for yourself." The portal suddenly activated but this time, it was black. Drake slowly entered the archway and into the portal, followed by Queen Evë. Drake opened his eyes and looked around. He was in a place he had never been at before.

"Where are we?" Drake asked.

"Moonshiar," Queen Evë answered.

"Is that where my friends are?"

"Yes." Suddenly, the ground started to shake. It shook the ground from one point on Evë and extended across the entire planet. Large clouds with blood-red lightning appeared above Mount Fire as the earthquake stopped. Then, he emerged from the top of the clouds. His laughter was the darkest of them all.

"Lord Taoî," Drake finally said.

"Yes," was all Queen Evë could say as the two stood there in pure shock. Then, everything went black. Drake saw a dim light in the distance and ran to it. He ran right into the light and before he knew it, he was on the other side of the archway. Queen Evë was standing next to it.

"What about my friends? Will they be okay?" he immediately asked as the portal closed.

"Yes, they will be fine. But, there is a cost for freeing your friends."

"What's that?"

"I do not know but I do know the location of the last stone. You need to go back to Tii. There, just outside of the town is a small drinking well. Use your powers to find the last stone."

"Okay," Drake said.

"Once you have the last stone, go to Father Brai's chambers. Inside, you'll need to find a device that will contact Father Paul. He will help you find the last artifact."

"The Tërcerlin Stone," Drake said.

"Once you have them, meet Christopher Anders as planned. He will deliver on his word, as promised," she continued, "you need to trust me."

"I do trust you and I won't let you down," he assured her as she started to fade.

"I know you won't," Queen Evë said. As she disappeared, she knew Drake wouldn't let her down because she knew he played a huge part in Lord Taoî's release. Just as Queen Evë had completely disappeared, the light around Drake got so bright that he had to cover his eyes. He was heading back to the real world. Nothing Drake could think of would work to change the future now. It was really all up to him to free his friends. But bad things were going to happen to Drake, and

Queen Evë was the only one who knew exactly what was going to happen next.

Chapter Nineteen:

To the Rescue

Drake ran as fast as he could down the path. He paused only to catch his breath then continued. He ran right past Lake Miir and before he knew it, he was on the outskirts of the Hill Lands. He came up to a fork in the road. It was the same one him, Zack, and Father John came to after they left what was left of Azel. He stood there, staring at the signs; in front of him was Deller's Pass and the Rocky Region, behind him was Lake Miir and the Eastern Mountains, to the right was the Hedia Mountains and Moonshiar, and to the left was the Hill Lands, the Northern Plains, and Jewel City.

Tears started to flood Drake's eyes. He quickly wiped them away because now, he was angry. Father John was murdered. He took off running forward as fast as he could, trying so hard not to stop until he got to the base of the Rocky Region. He barely made it there before he was about out of breath. As he was catching his breath, he looked around, trying to find Father John's body. He kept looking then shortly found a dirt mount in the form of a body. Flowers, though dying, were placed around the base of the mount. Drake fell to his knees at the end of the mount. He couldn't stop himself from crying.

"I'm so sorry Father John," he said, as though he was actually talking to him, "I'm sorry I didn't protect you. I should have been there. I should have been there to stop him; to stop you from dying." More tears streamed down his face. Suddenly, a small breeze blew in Drake's direction. It felt warm and comforting as it hit Drake. The small breeze seemed to circle Drake for a moment then suddenly dissipated. Drake took it as a sign that Father John would always be with him. He whipped away his tears and smiled.

"Thank you," he said. Drake stood up and walked away, heading to Tii. As Drake started his climb through the Rocky Region, evening fell. As he got closer to Tii, there were no sirens, no archers, nothing. He slowly walked up to the town.

"Hello?" he shouted as he started through the town, "hello? Is anyone there?" His voice echoed throughout the town, but no one responded. He found the well and examined it. Across the well, the wood looked ordinary. There were no engravings or burn marks; just worn away a bit by the weather. He looked down the well but all he saw was darkness. Drake walked around the well, counting six identical rounded stones, but which stone was the right stone? He slowly and carefully removed each stone and placed them all in a row. After for sure narrowing it down to two stones, Drake used the Light within him to choose the code stone. After placing the other stones back, he started to head when he found a small vial with a note attached to it. He looked at the vial then the note. USE WHEN NEEDED! it read. Drake had no idea what it was or what it was for but he kept it still. He got up and hurried to Father Brai's chambers.

Nighttime came and Drake barricaded the door, just in case. He started searching for the device that would contact Father Paul. As Drake searched, looking anywhere. All night long, he searched and searched but had no luck. The sky soon started to turn pink with the rising of the sun, and inside Drake was passed out on a chair, exhausted from all the searching.

"Hello?" came a quiet voice from somewhere inside the chambers. "Hello?" it said again. The hellos startled Drake awake. "Is this stupid thing even working?" the voice said. Drake immediately started searching again. "Hello?.... Hello? Father Brai, are you there?" As Drake got closer to the voice, the sound got louder until he found a golden box. "Hello?" the voice came from within the box. Drake placed the box on a table and opened it. Inside was a fairly large crystal square.

"Father Brai?" came the voice from the crystal square, "are you there? It's me, Father Paul."

"Hello? Hello?" Drake immediately shouted at the ball, trying to make contact. "Father Paul, can you hear me?"

"Yes," he answered, "but who are you and where is Father Brai?"

"He's….," Drake paused a moment, "he's been kidnapped."

"Kidnapped? By who?" Father Paul interrupted.

"Darkness," Drake said. Silence came over the ball. "Well, someone who's working for Darkness but just as bad."

"So who are you?"

"I'm Drake, Drake Shaw. But most people know me as 'The Chosen One'."

"Wait, 'THE Chosen One'?"

"The very one. But listen. This is extremely important!"

"Right," assured Father Paul.

"I was told you know where to find one of the five ancient artifacts. Is that true?"

"Well, I've never tested it but in theory, yes."

"Tested it? Tested what?" Drake asked, confused.

"Many years ago, I was on a walk one day when I stumbled upon a small, shallow pool. I went to take a drink from it when I noticed something stuck at the very bottom. I examined it and realized it was the Lost Soul of Möwatei. I rushed to get some equipment to carefully remove it but by the time I got back, it was gone."

"Mr. Anders," Drake said under his breath.

"I took a small sample of the pool water back. I've done several tests and I believe I may have found a way to find that artifact, or any other artifacts in close range."

"How does it work?"

"That is where my trouble came into play. I need an artifact to activate the locator spell."

"You're I'm luck. I have one of the Stones of Stones."

"That's perfect!" shouted Father Paul.

"But how do I get to you?" Drake asked.

"Why I'm in Crystral," he responded.

"Crystral?"

"Have you heard of Deller's Pass?"

"Umm....," Drake paused a moment to think. "Yeah, several people have told me of it."

"Excellent!" Father Paul said somewhat excited, "so what you need to do is come to Crystral so we can test my locator spell." Father Paul started laughing with excitement.

"Alright, I'm on my way," Drake said in a hurry.

"Right. Take Father Brai's communicator and contact me when you get to the shoreline. From there, I'll help you get across the sea."

"Okay," Drake replied, "see you soon." He closed the box. A sharp pain shot through Drake's stomach. Drake hadn't eaten in hours and boy, was he hungry.

"I'm sorry Father Brai," Drake said as he raided Father Brai's food. After becoming full, Drake packed up some food, grabbed the box, and headed for Crystral.

Drake hurried as fast as he could as often as he could. For every hour Drake didn't have that last artifact was another hour his friends were still being held hostage. It was still morning when he left but he only had until tomorrow at noon to have the other artifact. What if I can't find the last artifact? What are they doing to my friends? Are they okay at least? These questions seemed to fill Drake's mind with doubt.

Meanwhile, Kim, Jessica, Father Brai, and Oshwaia were chained to a wall, while Zack was chained inside of a steel cage. Mr. Anders and a few guards walked into the cellar.

"You won't get away with this," Father Brai said as he tried to break free.

"I already have," Mr. Anders replied. He walked up to Zack's cage. "You're the one I'm looking for," he said as he started to open it.

"What do you want with Zack?" Jessica quickly asked.

"I don't want him," he paused, "my master does."

"Who's your master?" Oshwaia asked.

"You'll see soon enough." Mr. Anders grabbed Zack and left the room, followed by the guards.

"Where do you think he is taking him?" Kim asked, scared beyond belief.

"I don't know," Oshwaia answered, "but I have a bad feeling about it." The four hung there, helpless and defenseless. Jessica closed her eyes and started concentrating. Kim started freaking out and tried to pull herself out of her chains but no luck. Father Brai looked for another way out but couldn't find one. Oshwaia just stood there motionless as though he gave up. The other three continued on but Jessica started concentrating harder. Little did she or anyone else know, she was actually melting the chains that were around her wrists. Suddenly, *CLANK CLANK*, the chains fell, freeing Jessica. She fell to her knees then slowly got up as she gathered her strength.

"How did you get free?" Kim asked as she suddenly stopped moving.

"Yeah," Father Brai responded.

"Like this," Jessica said as she closed her eyes and started concentrating again. *CLANK CLANK CLANK*. One by one, Kim, Father Brai, and Oshwaia were freed.

"How did you melt the chains?" Father Brai asked as he examined them.

"I'm not one hundred percent for sure but I closed my eyes and thought real hard about how I wanted to be free and suddenly, I was free."

"Hmmmmm….," Oshwaia said as he examined the melted chains as well.

"What?" she asked.

"I'll explain later," he said, "but first, we need to find Zack and the artifacts and then get out of here."

"I agree," Father Brai said. He slowly opened the door, revealing a staircase that led around the room heading upward. "Follow me," he said as he exited the room. The other three followed. At the top of the stairs was another door. Father Brai slowly opened the door, but only to find several soldiers with swords pointed at them with Mr. Anders standing behind them. Immediately, the four of them surrendered.

"Did you honestly think you could escape, especially from the powers of Darkness?" Mr. Anders said as he chuckled. Two soldiers suddenly ran down the stairs the four just came from.

"You'll never get away with this," Father Brai said determinedly, "Drake will stop you!" Mr. Anders stopped chuckling and a deeper voice started to chuckle from the shadows behind him. A figure suddenly appeared behind Mr. Anders. It walked forward, revealing a person. Fear struck the four right in the face.

"Drake won't be able to stop me," the man said.

"It's, it's, it's," Kim tried to say.

"It's Michael Cashner, at your service," he said as he chuckled even more. The two soldiers suddenly appeared from the stairs.

"They were melted sir," said one of the soldiers.

"You think magic can help you escape?" Mr. Cashner was near tears because he was laughing so hard.

"Where's Zack? What have you done with him?" Jessica bravely asked.

"Oh him? He'll be fine, seeing Drake holds up his end of the deal," Mr. Anders said as he laughed with Mr. Cashner.

"What should we do with them?" one of the soldiers asked. The two men stopped laughing.

"Take them to the temple's cell. Not even magic can help them there," Mr. Cashner demanded.

"Come," the same soldier said. The four knew they were beaten but still had hope that Drake would save them.

It was afternoon by the time Drake got to the shoreline. He quickly opened the box.

"Father Paul?" Drake said into the crystal square, "Are you there? It's Drake." There was no response. "Hello?" he paused, "Father Paul?"

"Drake? Drake, is that you?" Father Paul's voice finally rang from the square.

"Yes, yes it's me. I'm at the shoreline."

"Very good. Just hold tight okay?"

"Okay," Drake said, somewhat confused. Drake stood there holding the box, waiting. Suddenly, an orange light started to glow in front of Drake's feet. It began to move around Drake, spiraling upward and leaving a light-trail behind. As soon as the light reached the top of Drake's head, it formed a circle and suddenly the entire light grew so bright that Drake had to cover his eyes. Moments later, Drake opened his eyes and saw that he was no longer on the shoreline but inside what appeared to be a workshop of some sort. The light had magically disappeared and in one corner of the room was a man standing in front of a switch.

"Welcome," the man said as he approached Drake, "welcome to Crystral. You must be Drake." He grabbed Drake's hand and started shaking it.

"You must be Father Paul," Drake said, a bit nervously. "Oh, it's so wonderful to meet 'The Chosen One'. There is so much I want to know, oh and to show you and tell you and."

"Father Paul? My friends, including Father Brai is in terrible danger. We need to hurry," Drake kindly interrupted.

"Right," Father Paul agreed. He quickly hurried over to his workbench. He pulled out the last drawer and reached all the way to the back. He pulled out a small black box, placed it on the workbench, and closed the drawer. He opened the box. Inside was a small vial with a deep violet liquid.

"Is that," Drake started to ask.

"The locator spell, yes," Father Paul interrupted, "do you have the artifact?" Drake opened his bag and pulled out the stone. Father Paul cleared off some room on his workbench. Drake placed the stone on the bench. Carefully, Father Paul poured the liquid onto the stone. Suddenly the stone started glowing the same dark violet as the liquid. "If this works, it should create a beam of light, pointing us towards the closest artifact," Father Paul said as he emptied the last of the liquid.

"What happens when it finds an artifact?" Drake asked.

"When the beam of light hits the artifact, it will start glowing like this one is," Father Paul answered. Just then, a beam of light, still a deep violet color, started to shine from the stone. "This is it!" Father Paul said with excitement. He immediately started packing some of his items.

"What are you doing?" Drake asked.

"We have to go find that artifact, no?" replied Father Paul sarcastically.

"Oh yeah," Drake said as he watched Father Paul pack. Little did they know, the beam of light was shining directly towards Drake. "Uhhh, Father Paul?" Drake asked suddenly. Father Paul stopped packing and looked towards Drake, who was glowing deep violet, just like the stone. The beam of light purposefully struck Drake. Suddenly, the Tërcerlin symbol on Drake's hand began to glow deep violet.

"You're....you're....," Father Paul tried to say as he stood there in pure shock.

"The Tërcerlin Stone," Drake said in shock as well.

"The sixth artifact, but how can this be?" Father Paul asked, still shocked. Drake was just as shocked. First, he was 'The Chosen One' and now, he's an ancient artifact too? What more could fate have in-store for Drake? The glowing faded from both around Drake and the stone.

"There must be a mistake or something," Father Paul assumed, "I'll just quickly start working on what went wrong."

"Nothing went wrong," Drake replied.

"What?"

"Nothing went wrong."

"What do you mean?"

"When that beam of light struck me, I felt a power inside of me that I can't describe but I just know that my power is the Tërcerlin Stone," Drake said. Deep inside, Drake realized he was destined for more than just being 'The Chosen One'. He dreaded this realization the most.

"So what now?" Father Paul asked.

"We rest. Tomorrow, we will get Father Brai and my friends back," Drake said with determination.

That night, Drake had another nightmare. On one side stood all of Drake's friends including Mr. Anders, his men, and even Mr. Cashner. On the other side was Father Paul and himself. The four friends started walking forward as Drake, holding the last stone started walking forward too. The two groups crossed each other. Drake was now in the hands of Darkness. Suddenly, Drake woke up.

It was barely daylight and Drake knew he wouldn't be able to go back to sleep. It was going to be a very long day for Drake.

After packing a few items, Father Paul was finally ready to join Drake in his mission to get his friends back. They teleported out of Crystral and began the day heading down Deller's Pass.

"Do you have a plan at all?" Father Paul finally asked to break the silence.

"No, not yet," Drake lied. He really did have a plan but there was no way Father Paul would agree with it let alone allow Drake to go through with his plan.

"Oh," was all Father Paul could say. The trip through Deller's Pass seemed like it took forever. Once the two got to where they were supposed to be, Drake sat down and waited. Father Paul joined him. "Are we early?" he asked. Drake looked up and noticed the sun was about high noon.

"I'm not for sure honestly," Drake said, a bit concerned. Off in the distance, Drake spotted something. It was Mr. Anders and his men. Once they arrived, they got off their eglîmos. They also helped Drake's friends off of the eglîmos they were brought in on. There was Kim, Jessica, Father Brai, and Oshwaia, but no Zack.

"Where's Zack?" Drake asked Mr. Anders determinedly. He started chuckling.

"Oh him?" he finally said.

"Where is Zack?" Drake was starting to get angry.

"He's right here," came a voice from behind Drake. Drake quickly spun around, only to find more men and with Zack and Mr. Cashner.

"Michael Ca," Drake started to say.

"Cashner," Mr. Cashner said as he started laughing. Drake turned his focus towards Zack, who was in the form of a silver wolf but had chains around his ankles and some kind of collar around his neck.

"Are you okay buddy?" Drake asked him.

"Yeah, I think so," Zack thought. Drake took a step towards Zack.

"Ah ah ah, the artifacts first," Mr. Anders said. Drake turned back around.

"And how do I know you're going to release ALL of my friends?" he asked.

"You have our word," Mr. Anders lied as he placed one hand over his heart. With a deep sigh, Drake pulled out the last Stone of Stones.

"Don't do it Drake," Father Brai said.

"Quiet you!" Mr. Cashner snapped at Father Brai who immediately silenced himself. He turned towards Drake. "The artifacts?" he asked. Drake turned around and handed the stone to Mr. Cashner.

"Where's the last artifact?" he demanded.

"I am the last artifact," Drake slowly said as he held out his hand and showed Mr. Cashner the Tërcerlin symbol. Mr. Cashner took his free hand and grabbed Drake by the neck, lifting him up.

"Drake!" Kim shouted as his five friends watched his struggle for air.

"Hmmmm," was all Mr. Cashner could say. Then, he let go of Drake, dropping him to the ground. Drake fell, gasping for air.

"Let them go!" he ordered. Kim, Jessica, Father Brai, and Oshwaia were released and freed except Zack.

"What....what....what about....Zack?" Drake asked while still trying to catch his breathe.

"Change in plans," Mr. Cashner said with an evil grin. He knelt down next to Drake. "He's not who he seems to be," he whispered to Drake. He looked at Mr. Cashner with confusion.

"What do you mean?" he asked. Instead of answering, Mr. Cashner just laughed then BAM, unconscious.

Chapter Twenty:

Darkness Is Coming

As Drake woke up, he quickly noticed his hands and feet were attached to a circular device. He was inside the device, which seemed to be hanging in midair. One wire ran from the device to another room and another wire ran to a control box that was directly in front of him. Standing on the opposite side of the control box was Mr. Cashner.

"I need the power of the Tërcerlin Stone you have inside of you," he said.

"What do you mean? What are you going to do to me?" Drake demanded to know. Mr. Cashner had an evil grin on his face, but didn't answer. Instead, he flipped a switch on the control box. Blood-red lightning came from the circular device, striking only Drake. Pain shot through his entire body, forcing him to scream. More and more lightning came out of the device, striking Drake. Each time a bolt struck him, he screamed harder due to the increase of pain. Then, blackness.

"Drake?" Zack licked Drake's face, "Drake? Are you okay?" he licked some more. "Drake?" Drake slowly started to wake up.

"Zack, is that you?" Drake said as his eyesight was still coming into focus.

"Yes! Yes Drake! It's me!" Zack thought delightfully, knowing Drake was okay. Drake gave Zack a huge hug.

"Where are we?" Drake asked as he slowly got up.

"I'm not sure," Zack walked up to a hole, "but I found a way out."

"Way to go Zack!" Drake said with a bit of happiness. He hurried over to the hole. "Let's get out of here."

"Yeah!" Zack agreed. Drake went into the hole first, followed by Zack. Before the two knew it, they were just outside Moonshiar. It was just about nightfall when the two climbed out of the hole.

"Come on, let's go!" Drake said quietly then started running away from Moonshiar. Zack followed behind. Moonshiar was still insight when the largest earthquake ever started. It shook the ground from one point on Evë and extended across the entire planet. Large clouds with blood-red lightning appeared above Mount Fire as the earthquake stopped. Then, he emerged from the top of the clouds. His eyes were as pitch as black, his bone covered clothing screamed death all over, and his laughter was the darkest of them all. Lord Taoî was again free....

Meanwhile, Father Paul made a wonderful feast for everyone, everyone except Drake and Zack, who they thought was still captured. All of their friends were gathered around the table about to eat when the ground started shaking. Just as it started, it stopped.

"What was that?" Father Brai asked. No one had a clue what was going on. They started eating but all of them knew something wasn't right.

Zack ran as fast as he could with Drake on his back.

"I'm really starting to see why you like this wolf form so much," Drake said. Zack only ran faster. Soon, the shoreline was insight. Once the two got there, Drake insisted that Zack rest to gain his strength but Zack didn't care. He ran right up to the shoreline then stopped.

"You ready?" he asked Drake.

"Ready for what?" Drake asked. Zack then transformed into a visnu. Drake took a deep breath and into the water they went. A few moments later, the two surfaced next to Crystral. Sirens started going off. Several guards were heading towards Drake and Zack. When they arrived, they drew their swords and pointed them at the two.

"State your business," a guard said.

"I need to speak with Father Paul at once! This matter is extremely important!" Drake replied ergently.

"Drake? Is that really you?" Father Paul said as he pushed his way through the guards. He was followed by everybody else.

"Drake!" shouted Kim as she darted for him as both Father Paul and Father Brai helped the two out of the water and gave him a hug, not caring he was wet.

"What happened to you?" Father Brai asked? A guard handed Drake a towel to dry off with. Zack transformed into a silver wolf and just shook himself dry.

"That's not important right now," Drake started off, "Lord Taoî has been released." A terrifying silence quickly flooded over everyone. "Darkness is coming and we need to find shelter."

"Can't we just stop him?" a guard asked.

"He's too strong. No one can defeat him," Drake responded.

"The labyrinth," Oshwaia said. "If we can get everyone into the labyrinth, I know a spell we can use to block all the entrances from Darkness."

"That's perfect!" Drake agreed. Everyone else did too because it seemed to be their only hope.

As morning came, every single person from Crystral, including Drake and his friends, Prince Evergreen and Father Izea, Jane Florence and the Azel survivors, and anyone else they could find were all gathering in front of the library in Jewel City. Once everyone was inside, Drake held out his hand to activate the way into the labyrinth like before but nothing happened. Drake lowered his hand and tried again. Still nothing. Suddenly, the ground started shaking like it did when Lord Taoî was released. Drake and his friends hurried outside, only to see that Darkness was heading their way. Panic broke out in the crowd. Drake hurried inside. He knew deep inside of him he still had his powers. He held out his hand one last time and just like before, the Tërcerlin symbol on the ground started to glow, the ground started to shake, and the entrance started to open, revealing the same staircase as before.

"Quickly!" Drake shouted to the crowd as the rounded wall came to a stop. Everyone hurried as fast as they could down the stairs. The last person to head down was Drake. He took one step onto the staircase but was grabbed and thrown backwards. It was Mr. Cashner. Suddenly, the entrance started to close.

"Looks like you're not going to make it," Mr. Cashner sneered.

"Watch me!" Drake said as he pulled out his sword. As the two started their fight, Darkness had finally reached the city's walls. Drake managed to shove Mr. Cashner at the right moment, forcing him to lose his balance and fall. Drake took a huge leap and barely made it before the labyrinth's entrance closed and just as Darkness entered the library, covering it.

On the stairs, Drake sat in complete darkness. He thought to himself that that was it. Darkness has won and he was finally defeated for good.

"Don't give up," came Queen Evë's voice from inside Drake's heart. The Tёrcerlin symbol on Drake's hand started to glow, giving him hope. Determination appeared on Drake's face as the light grew, because it was at that moment that he realized that Darkness might have won this battle, but the war was far from over....

To be continued....

www.ingramcontent.com/pod-product-compliance
Lightning Source LLC
Chambersburg PA
CBHW060857250626
47159CB00008B/2776